An Idea About My Dead Uncle

A Novel

GUERNICA
PRIZE
1

Canada Council   Conseil des Arts
for the Arts   du Canada

ONTARIO ARTS COUNCIL
CONSEIL DES ARTS DE L'ONTARIO

an Ontario government agency
un organisme du gouvernement de l'Ontario

Canadä

Guernica Editions Inc. acknowledges the support of the Canada Council
for the Arts and the Ontario Arts Council. The Ontario Arts Council
is an agency of the Government of Ontario.

We acknowledge the financial support of the Government of Canada.

An Idea About My Dead Uncle

 A Novel

K.R. Wilson

GUERNICA
EDITIONS
TORONTO • BUFFALO • LANCASTER (U.K.)
2019

Michael Mirolla, editor
David Moratto, cover and Interior design
Guernica Editions Inc.
1569 Heritage Way, Oakville, (ON), Canada L6M 2Z7
2250 Military Road, Tonawanda, N.Y. 14150-6000 U.S.A.
www.guernicaeditions.com

Distributors:
University of Toronto Press Distribution,
5201 Dufferin Street, Toronto (ON), Canada M3H 5T8
Gazelle Book Services, White Cross Mills
High Town, Lancaster LA1 4XS U.K.

First edition.
Printed in Canada.

Legal Deposit—Third Quarter
Library of Congress Catalog Card Number: 2018968308
Library and Archives Canada Cataloguing in Publication
Title: An idea about my dead uncle : a novel / K.R. Wilson.
Names: Wilson, K. R., 1958- author.
Description: Series statement: Guernica prize ; 1.
Identifiers: Canadiana (print) 20190045086 | Canadiana (ebook)
20190045094 | ISBN 9781771834513 (softcover) | ISBN 9781771834520
(EPUB) | ISBN 9781771834537 (Kindle)
Classification: LCC PS8645.I4695 I34 2019 | DDC C813/.6—dc23

*To my remarkable wife
and our outstanding daughter*

Dear soul, if you were not friends
with the vast nothing inside,
why would you always be casting your net
into it, and waiting so patiently?
—Rumi, *Craftsmanship and Emptiness* (trans. Coleman Barks)

Contents

PART I

One

I HAVE AN IDEA. ABOUT MY DEAD UNCLE.

A chamber opera. Small ensemble, maybe some electronics. Four or five singers doing multiple roles.

No, wait, hear me out.

Uncle Larry went to China when I was five and never came back. We don't even know for sure that he's dead. It's a great story. Or would be, I imagine. If we actually knew what it was.

I just have bits so far: a made-up narrative arc for the second act, a melody half-cribbed from some incidental music that I wrote about five years ago for a local theatre company. An ethereal harmonic progression that I'm sure I'll find a place for. It wants to happen. It nags me in the night, sends me creeping to the kitchen table with a notepad or some music paper just to empty out my head so I can sleep.

Louisa never stirs, even if I'm up three or four times.

We pretty much assume that he's dead, after twenty-five years. Or most of us do.

He isn't even my uncle, really. He's Mama's cousin. Or was, if he's dead. Aunt Jasmine believes he's still alive, but then I guess a mother has to. If he is, though, you'd think he'd have contacted someone by now, no matter how hard it may have been to get letters out of China in the 70s. Or especially now, with the Internet. You'd think he'd have contacted Aunt Jasmine at least.

I used to sneak over to her place sometimes for tea and pastries, and the occasional family story. Stories from Mama's side, that I wasn't supposed to want to know about. She makes these great little pastries called moon cakes. Mama never made moon cakes. Mama was never allowed to make anything Chinese. There were a lot of rules for Mama.

I remember one day she was supposed to mow the lawn, but didn't. When Dad got home she was asleep on the kitchen floor. I had cleaned up the spills and put the empties under the sink, but I couldn't get her to wake up, to wash her face, to sit in a chair. I was probably six or seven. He twisted her arm up behind her back until she cried and pushed her out to the shed. She mowed the lawn one-handed, rocking the mower from side to side to turn it around at the end of each row. Her arm was in a sling for four days.

Oh, for a while we sometimes went out for Chinese food, but only the same way that we sometimes went out for steak or spaghetti. When we got to go out at all. There was a little place with chrome and Arborite tables in a strip mall on Macleod Trail that served "Chinese and Canadian Cuisine," the menu neatly segregated: egg rolls and chow mein on the left, burgers and club sandwiches on the right. I could always tell if Teresa was trying to suck up to Dad by which side she ordered from.

Dad always had the roast beef sandwich *au jus*. I can still see him turning his head sideways to bite into the gristly folds of meat, into the darkened bun dripping with what he always called "the awe juice." Mama usually had coffee and rice. Plain white rice. It wasn't licenced, the Chinese food place. I was often the only one who ventured into the mysterious realms of chop suey and sweet and sour pork, or chicken balls in their sticky scarlet goo.

For a while.

But suppose he *is* still alive?

I've mentioned the opera-in-progress to a handful of my music acquaintances, but they just smile the way you smile at a five-year-old who says he's going to be a fireman. The smiles are kind, but I see it all in their eyes. *Waste of time and talent. No chance of it ever getting produced. Who besides Wagner writes their own libretto anyhow?* Plus I think they've had me a little pigeonholed since last year when the CBC included *Infernal Variations (String Trio), by Jason Lavoie* on a CD of works by regional Asian-Canadian composers.

I'm Jason Lavoie, in case that wasn't clear. La-*voy*, by the way, not La-*vwa*. Dad was always very insistent about that, and by now the habit is worked in too deep to get rid of, even though I get grief about it from people like Bill Bonenfant, the cellist from St. Albert who played on the recording. But that's how it plays when you've been assimilated anglophones for multiple generations. Linguistic fidelity is fine for the folks in St. Albert, or in the towns south of the rail line in Saskatchewan, but here in Calgary it's just considered snooty.

Like *Bill* is such a traditional franco name.

I have mixed feelings about even being on that disc. I hate playing the Asian card. I just want to be seen as a composer, not as some exotic sub-type. But hey, would you turn down a chance to be recorded?

It's the part after he gets to China that's troublesome, of course, especially since he probably spends about three-quarters of the opera there. There were only a few early letters, and no-one heard from him again once they stopped, so I pretty much have to make it all up. I have to base it on my general sense of him and on what I know about China, which is tricky, since he left when I was five and I know virtually nothing about China. So I'm mostly working on the music at this point.

I'm sitting at my keyboard—a Korg M1 I bought used about a year ago—trying to construct a quasi-heroic melody in the tenor range. I see Uncle Larry as a tenor, struggling for reform in the middle of a chorus of baritone bureaucrats. I have the headphones on to avoid disturbing Louisa, so I don't hear her come in to bring me a coffee. She's just suddenly there, reaching around me toward the side table where my manuscript paper is, and I twitch with surprise.

"Sorry," she says. "Didn't mean to startle you."

She sets the coffee down on a coaster and places a settling hand on my shoulder. She leans forward and peers at the manuscript. Across the top staff of a six-stave line are three bars of melody and about eight bars of eraser smudges. The other staves—intended for a three-part men's chorus of bureaucrats and a piano score that I won't orchestrate until later—are blank. At this point I have no idea who the bureaucrats are, or why they're there, or what they have to say, or even if they're historically accurate. I just like the image.

"What do you think of this?" I ask. I turn on the little amplifier that connects the Korg to the bookshelf speakers and play her the three bars of melody, half-singing along to illustrate that it's a vocal line. It doesn't seem like much for two hours' work.

"Hmmm," she says. She touches a knuckle to her lower lip. She's not being evasive. She has a reasonable sense of modern music, especially after living with me for—Jesus, is it really more than four years now?—and she'll give me a real opinion. It's probably just too small a sample to get much of a grip on.

"You have to imagine it kind of rising up above this chorus of bureaucrats," I say, making a rising motion with my hand, fingers curled upward as if in struggle.

"Oka-a-ay," she says, as if letting that notion sink in. "And what will the chorus sound like?"

I shake my head. "No idea."

I put my arm around her hips. She kisses the top of my head.

I remember Mama tapping the coffee scoop against the inside of the tin, to get it level before tipping it into the paper cone. I remember her hair, dead black in the living room sun, as she picked out tunes on the piano with one hand. Old MacDonald. Twinkle twinkle. Canadian tunes, they might have said, at the restaurant with the chrome tables. I remember moisture in the fold at the corner of her eye.

She didn't drink every day, at least not then. Then it was only on the weekend, and sometimes not even until the afternoon. But it was enough, especially on the odd occasion when it spilled into public view. Staggering down the front walk to the car. Overbalancing while reaching for the morning *Albertan* and tumbling down the front steps.

It was plenty.

Mama sometimes said I had some special connection with Uncle Larry, but that she never understood what it was. I wonder now how much of that was bullshit.

The not understanding, I mean.

I remember a day in Banff. It's hard to say how much is actual memory and how much is based on Mama's whispered retellings, but it seems remarkably clear to me. It was one of the last times — maybe *the* last time — that anyone from Mama's side joined an outing with Uncle Mark's family. I stuck close to Uncle Larry the whole time. It wasn't very long before he left for China. I must have been around four.

We were walking down Banff Avenue on our way to some lunch place after a soak in the hot pool. My hair still smelled like sulphur. It was fun once I was in — the delicious contrast between the hot-spring water and the chill of the outdoor air, the strangeness of swimming surrounded by snow — but at first I was scared to wade through the little curtain of clear plastic strips between the change room and the pool. Uncle Mark yelled at me for holding everyone up, and called me something bad. Mama seemed about to say something, but stopped. Dad didn't even start. Uncle Larry took my hand and guided me through, holding the strips aside as I passed.

On Banff Avenue there were funny signs in some of the store

windows. I was too young to know what they were, or probably even to notice them, but my cousin Danny must have been old enough to realize that they were Asian characters of some kind. He would have been about six.

"Hey Jason," he said, with a twisted little smirk. "What does *that* say?" And then he laughed, looking up at his Dad. Auntie Jill shushed him, but Uncle Mark laughed a little too.

Two stores later there was another sign, and Danny said: "Hey Jason, what does *that* one say?" Same smirk, cranked up a notch.

"Danny, shush," Auntie Jill said, scowling down at him.

"Leave the kid alone," Uncle Mark said. "It's a joke, for Christ's sake."

He was talking to Auntie Jill.

I remember feeling small and prickly, knowing that Danny was somehow beating me at a game I didn't get. I took Uncle Larry's hand.

"It's Japanese, not Chinese," Uncle Larry said. "Japanese tourists love the mountains."

Uncle Mark grunted something nasty.

"Some of the characters are the same as in Chinese, though," Uncle Larry went on. He didn't know Uncle Mark very well. "The Japanese borrowed them from us."

"Well they should give 'em back," Uncle Mark said with a snort. "Get some new ones people can actually *read*." And he gave Uncle Larry a smile that I knew was mean, and was meant to be mean.

After that I got whiny about walking, and Uncle Larry put me on his shoulders. Then Mama spotted the restaurant a couple blocks ahead, and pointed it out. Then Danny saw another sign.

"Hey Jason," he said. By now he was practically dancing with delight at his own wit, in the glow of his father's endorsement. "What does *that* one say?"

Uncle Larry turned his face up toward mine and whispered something. I missed it. He whispered it again.

"Fur coats," I said.

Danny's dance-step slowed a little. Half a block later he asked his question again, and again there was a whisper from Uncle Larry.

"Stone carvings," I said.

And after that there were no more questions.

Danny started picking on his sister instead. Auntie Jill shushed him, and this time Uncle Mark shushed him too. He was sullen right through lunch. Uncle Larry sat across from me and smiled.

I had a hamburger and french fries.

Two

I TAKE THE LRT IN TO WORK FOR ABOUT QUARTER TO SIX, SINCE IT'S my turn to open. The first thing I always do is put on the music. Bach again today. We're supposed to play this corporate mix of old jazz and country pop, but especially during the quiet times of the day I play what I like, and at least once or twice a week that means Bach. I managed to get in all of Stravinsky's *Symphony of Psalms* last Thursday during the lull between the stroller brigade and the lunch crowd, since I'm on a bit of a Stravinsky kick at the moment, but that was unusual. Mostly I try to hit that narrow band where my own tastes overlap with what the customers will tolerate without scowling.[1]

This morning it's the *Motets*, BWV 225-230. I take the CD from my backpack, load it into the sound system and fire up the last one, *Lobet den Herrn, alle Heiden*, which I particularly like. There's something soothing about Bach's mathematically precise control over interacting voices. Webern has some of that same level of control, but I'd never get away with playing him here.

Humming along with occasional bits of the soprano line I unlock the cash registers and get the steam building in the espresso machines.

---

1. The *Symphony of Psalms* was actually a nod in that direction, since my Stravinsky kick is more about his more savage stuff like *The Rite of Spring* than his neoclassical stuff. I'm not sure why that is. Knowing me, it should be the other way around. Maybe I'm *evolving.*

I cut the binding from the stack of today's *Heralds* and *Globes* and square them up in the wire rack near the door. At about ten to six I start coffee brewing in three of the drip machines—one dark, one mild, one decaf—so it'll be ready when the customers start coming in, and I chalk the names of the blends on the board on the wall. I wipe down the counters and the little round tables and brush any lingering pastry crumbs from the armchairs.

Just as the CD starts over, with *Singet dem Herrn ein neues Lied*, the first of my counter staff, the geology student, turns up, and I let him in. I've got him here early today because he has afternoon classes on Wednesdays. The next one, who sings in an alt-metal band, is in at seven because she has a show tonight and can't do the afternoon, and the single dad has the afternoon shift because that's when his mom can take over looking after his kid.

Scheduling is actually something that the manager is supposed to do rather than the assistant (me), but he finds it overwhelming and usually screws it up. I offered to do it the day after the single dad's ten-month old had to spend half a shift behind the counter in her stroller, and I've been doing it ever since. Thank Christ she's a good sleeper.

At six I unlock the outside door. There's already a small line-up of commuters waiting, a couple with their own insulated mugs. I work the register and draw the drip coffee while the geology student looks after the espresso drinks.

When the alt-metal singer comes in at seven she takes over for me behind the counter. I sit at the computer in the closet-sized office to update the inventory and sales stats and to pick up the latest marketing directions from head office in Vancouver. We're adding whole grain bagels to the menu next quarter. There's a PDF diagram showing how to rearrange the cooler to make space for them.

"Jason," I remember Mama snapping, "I said that's enough goddamn jam!" I was probably six or seven. She grabbed the jar, and my table knife, still half inside, flipped up out of my hand and hit the wall behind me, leaving a small strawberry gouge. As the knife clattered to the kitchen floor she stood staring at this new burden — the cleaning, the patching, the explaining — her face quivering between anger and disbelief. Then the quivering stopped, draining away, it seemed, into the linoleum, and she fell limply back into her chair. She set the jam jar down like a drink, beside the drink that was already there.

I picked my moment, gambling that she was too stunned to react. "When I'm grown up," I said, "I'm going to buy a jar of jam and eat the whole thing with a spoon."

"You do that," she said flatly, her hand sliding from the jar to the glass.

At ten I slide back the curtain of narrow Plexiglas panels that separates the coffee bar from the warehouse-sized bookstore. I actually started out in the bookstore, but it turned out that the money was marginally better behind the coffee counter. It's run by a separate chain.

If you're a twentysomething composer in Calgary without a university degree, you don't pay the bills with your art. Having either soured on or failed at warehouse work, telemarketing and door-to-door vinyl siding sales, these days I pour coffee.

Oh, all right, I'm making it more bleak than it is. I get an additional seventy cents an hour to help manage six other coffee-pourers too.

I was assistant conductor of a small church choir for a while, but the hours were short, the pay was crap, I got all of the shit jobs (like doing drills with the four enthusiastic but worse-than-average tenors — two of whom were really squeezed up baritones — to try to get them to sound less like gut-shot ducks and more like, say tenors), and I hated getting up early on Sundays. Plus there was the whole not-believing-in-God thing. But at least it was a music job, and better than teaching piano lessons, which I lasted at for six weeks before

I realized that making eight-year-olds cry in humiliation wasn't effective pedagogy.

The coffee thing pays better, though. And when I do music, it's mine.

The manager is on from two until closing, so I have the evening off, which he wasn't initially happy about but I needed it. I recently did the music and sound design for a church-basement production by a local amateur theatre group—which I still do from time to time if I'm asked—and in return they gave me four tickets to the opening performance. That was about all they could afford. I have mixed feelings about the show—it's a slight bedroom farce where the wit occasionally rises to *double entendres* on the word 'coming,' plus the actors aren't all that good—but hey, a night out is a night out.

We're meeting my friend Miranda and her husband for dinner first, at some soybean-and-wheatgrass place where the servers all have hemp sandals and tongue studs and vermilion-streaked hair. Louisa and I arrive first. A tiny, tattooed blond girl seats us at an unfinished cedar table, its edges worn dark and smooth by generations of unbleached cotton sleeves, and leaves us a stack of photocopied menus in thin plastic covers. One side is entirely juices.

I've known Miranda since we were both in first year. She was a clarinet student with a keener-than-usual interest in new music, and played in my first official student production—a relentlessly uneventful series of sustained consonances for wind instruments and accordion called *Satori*. I meant it to sound kind of timeless, but in hindsight it was just tedious.

We got along so well during rehearsals—in stark contrast with myself and Phil, the humourless accordionist who seemed to take almost any comment as a slight against his instrument[2]—that we started hanging out a little between classes, and then going with

---

2. Which was really unnecessary, since I actually found it a pleasure to write for.

small groups of other first-years for coffee or for beers at Mac Hall, or to cheap movies at the Plaza. Then one night during a showing of *Walkabout* I casually and—I thought—quite naturally, rested my hand on her knee, and she jerked away so sharply the harpsichord player on her other side bounced some popcorn down her own cleavage.

During the walk back to the CTrain afterward I managed to separate her from the herd for a moment.

"Did I do something wrong?"

Her hands were deep in her pockets, her eyes on the sidewalk. "No. Um. Maybe. No, I just. I mean. Oh shit, forget it."

"OK," I said. "It's fine. Really."

And somehow it was. We never talked about it again, and never needed to. And we stayed friends.

She teaches at Mount Royal now, and plays in a pretty good semi-professional woodwind quintet, and the Calgary Philharmonic calls her up whenever they're performing one of those grotesque post-Wagnerian symphonies that calls for fifteen or twenty of each wind instrument. Her husband does something in the oil patch.

They arrive just as our lip-studded server is bringing my shade-grown fair trade coffee and Louisa's grapefruit and carrot juice.

"Sorry we're a little late," Miranda says with a wry *it wasn't me* look. "We got a *little* caught up in the Y2K planning." She pulls out one of the mismatched chairs and sits.

Her husband is defensive. "It's not a hoax, you know. Shit could really go down." He sits next to her.

"Well, if it does, we certainly have enough collapsible eight-gallon water containers now." Not looking up from the menu, but smiling.

"How many?" I ask. The straight man.

"Only six," Miranda's husband says, a wrinkle of disappointment across his brow.

"Only," Miranda says, looking at me. Absolutely deadpan.

"You'd be surprised how quickly forty-eight gallons might go," her husband says. Married I don't know how many years now and he sometimes still can't tell when she's winding him up for sport. "Between basic drinking water, reconstituting the freeze-dried meals—"

"How many of those?" I ask Miranda.

"Six cases. Mountain Equipment Co-op." She turns away from her husband so he can't see the corners of her mouth twitching. "Hiker food."

"Never mind," he says. "You'll be thanking me on New Year's Day." He leans across to me. "How are your preparations coming, Jason?"

"Um. Well," I say. "We've, ah … I think we've got a couple of cans of chili in the pantry." Louisa and Miranda both snicker.

And then Miranda's husband gives me a look that is so earnest, and so frightened, and so goddamn, I don't know, so goddamn *mobilized*, that suddenly I feel like blowing off the play and heading straight for Mountain Equipment Co-op myself, right now, right this minute.

Jesus. My back is even covered in cold sweat.

It's Miranda who pulls me back. "Hey, Y2K will be a big milestone for you, I guess."

"Yeah," Louisa says, linking her arm through mine. She sometimes gets a touch territorial around Miranda, which I've never quite understood. "The three-oh," she says warmly, looking up at me with a soft smile.

I was a 1970 New Year's Baby. Not *the* New Year's Baby. I was born an hour and forty-seven minutes too late for that honour. But *a* New Year's Baby nonetheless. That means, of course, that my thirtieth will coincide with all of the new millennium crap. Hurray for me.

"Yeah, hurray for me," I say. "The whole world will be celebrating my milestone birthday in grand goddamn style."

"Or sliding back to the pre-information age," Miranda's husband says. Without apparent irony. And there's that sweat down my back again.

And it stays there as kind of an undercurrent through the course of the meal, which probably accounts for the slight stink that I raise toward the end when our server tells me that they're out of the organic strawberry ice cream. Later on, though, when the play slightly exceeds my admittedly low expectations—decently acted, with a couple of actual out-loud laughs that hadn't jumped out at me from the script—the cold sweat starts to seem kind of silly. A couple of weird moments at dinner, is all. Low blood sugar or something.

And yet as we pass a hardware store on our way back to the car, I find myself looking in through the darkened window for chemical toilets and propane stoves.

It's late when we get home but the opera is crying for attention again, so while Louisa drops her pocket change into the Montreal Bucket and washes her face and brushes her teeth and changes into her tartan flannel nightshirt, I settle in at the Korg with my headphones and my pencil and work pretty much fruitlessly until almost dawn.

I have a split shift the next day, opening the store at eight and closing it at eleven that night, which gives me a big but circumscribed gap in the middle. These gaps never feel like down time. The return to work is always hanging there. Plus I end up spending the whole day in my uniform, since I don't want to waste the time going all the way home and back to change.[3] Today it's the mint-green golf shirt with the company logo on the pocket. I'd bitch to whoever did up the uniform schedule, but that'd be me. Sometimes it just can't be helped.

During my long mid-day break I go visit Uncle Mark. There is always a sour smell in the hallway I can never identify. Maybe it's just the natural odour of old people gathered together out of the

---

3. Though it occurs to me now that I write it down that I could always bring a change of shirt with me in my bag. Seems kind of obvious now, actually.

way. A few wheelchairs are coming toward me on their way to lunch. The Gnarled Man with the Plaid Blanket. The Balding Woman. The One who Always Smiles. I weave past them to Uncle Mark's room.

Uncle Mark kidnapped me three days after I was born.

He didn't bring me back for a week.

He's sitting in a clunky black wheelchair, his shoulders at an odd angle and his hands in his lap. He's up. A good day, maybe.

"Uncle Mark?" Pause. "Uncle Mark?"

He used to throw me in the air and then catch me, laughing at the fear in my mother's eyes. He once pulled up a tree stump in our back yard with nothing but a block-and-tackle and the strength in his back. Now girls in polyester pastels hold up his jaw while he drinks beige meal-replacement through a bendy straw.

"Uncle Mark? It's Jason."

His skin is thin and finely wrinkled, his hair askew, his tangled eyebrows littered with flakes of skin. There are thick purple bruises along his forearms and the backs of his hands. As I settle into the guest chair his eyes come into rough focus near my face.

Two strokes eight months ago stole his speech, but he tries anyhow, his mouth struggling around the husks of half-remembered words. *Mmmmmm, hhhhhhhh, hhhhhhhaaaaaaaah* he says, and looks at me expectantly. I shake my head. "Sorry," I say. "Didn't get that." He makes a few pointed gestures with a twisted, root-like hand toward—well, toward what exactly? The wall? The reception desk outside? The mountains in the distance?—and tries again. *Hnhhhhhh. Mmmmmmhhh. Anhhhhhh.* Gesture. *Anhhhhh.* Gesture. *Anhhhhhh.* I have no idea what he's trying to say.

"OoooOOOOooh *God!*" A wavering male voice from down the hall interrupts. "OooOOOoooh, Jesus *Christ.*"

Teresa once said it was for blood tests. The kidnapping. Paternity tests. Me, I'm not so sure. I think there must have been more to it. But I don't know what, and now it's too late to ask.

"I brought you some music too. Something I wrote. It's on a CD."

Maybe he understands. Maybe not. I put it in the boxy black stereo on the window ledge and cue up the string trio. Maybe he's listening. Maybe not. He seems to notice when the music stops, which I guess is something. But maybe not such a good day after all.

I'm not sure why I visit Uncle Mark. Not that I do it often, mind you, but we weren't exactly close. I guess at first it was a *ha ha, you poisonous bastard, let's see you smack me now* kind of thing. But by now it feels like something else.

Late in the afternoon I give Sleeve a call at work. He's an up-and-comer at the York and Empire Bank, working up personal financial plans for low-end rich folks. How to cover the kids' university and still buy a boat when you retire, that sort of thing. He started as a teller right after his economics degree and he's been climbing the ladder ever since, always doing some evening course on derivatives, or rollovers, or how to mortify your consanguination returns.

It's odd to see someone as wildly inconsiderate as Sleeve thrive in a circumspect service industry like banking, but I guess the right combination of math smarts and rock-solid scrupulousness can offset even Sleeve-grade prickitude.

Sleeve transferred to our Junior High from a school in Edmonton about a month into Grade 8. He was late his first day. We were already in second period, Social Studies,[4] when he came crashing in through the door at the back, his scuffed leather jacket hanging half off one shoulder, his backpack slipping down to his elbow. Mrs. Thickson stopped speaking and looked up over her reading glasses. She glanced down at the class list on her desk, then back up at Sleeve.

"Are you Mr. ... Sloo-ka?" she asked.

He looked up from shrugging his backpack onto the seat of a

---

4. We were studying apartheid. Isn't it funny the things you remember?

vacant desk and scowled. "*Sleeve*-ka," he said. There was a don't-fuck-with-me edge to his voice.

A couple of guys laughed, but I didn't. Here was someone who cared how his name was pronounced. Cared enough to challenge a teacher. On his first day of school. Before he'd even taken off his coat.

I liked this guy already.

Sleeve and I drifted together gradually, through a series of small things we had in common. We were both late picks for lunch hour football. We were both reading *The Name of the Rose*. We were both fairly average students—except for Sleeve in math, where he was some kind of prodigy. We were both regularly baited by the tough guys who smoked cigarettes in the side doorway. ("*Slee-eeeeve*-ka.") We were both reluctant to talk about our fathers. Sleeve in particular.

By the end of the second semester I found out why.

We'd been in on a mucky, ill-tempered game of pick-up softball under a damp spring sky, but as soon as each of us had struck out once, the team captains started skipping us in the batting order, so we picked up our backpacks and wandered off along the chain link fence.

Sleeve seemed unusually preoccupied. He wasn't saying much, just walking. Then he suddenly kicked out sideways at the fence, rattling it all the way back to the diamond. Carl Rich, the captain of the team Sleeve had been on, looked up at the sound and took a pitch to the shoulder.[5] A few steps farther along Sleeve kicked the fence again, even harder.

---

5. After high school Carl ended up selling carpet at a chain store in Midnapore. He had a wispy moustache and a mullet, and wore black basketball shoes with his suits. Two winters ago he ran his car off the Calf Robe Bridge and bled to death before the paramedics could get him out. I'm not saying it's some kind of karma for being a prick in junior high or anything, and he doesn't even have anything to do with the rest of this story. It's just that I haven't thought about him in a while and suddenly this thing about Sleeve brings him back, you know?

"Listen, fuck Retch," I said. "Why would we give a shit about their shitty little ball game anyhow?"

"I don't give a shit about Retch, or his fucking game," Sleeve said. He kicked the fence again, harder still.

"So what, then?" I said, gesturing toward the fence.

But Sleeve didn't say anything, he just kept walking. He stopped kicking the fence, though.

When we got to the end of the fence he kept on going, off the school grounds and toward the 7-Eleven two blocks down. I stayed with him. He bought a Mountain Dew and a bag of Old Dutch ripple chips and we sat on the curb. He held out the chip bag without looking at me, just staring down at the road, and I took a couple. For a while we just sat there and ate chips, not talking. And then he did.

"My Dad's getting out this weekend."

I had no idea what he was talking about.

"Out of where?"

He took a swig of his Mountain Dew. "Drumheller."

"Drumheller?" I was puzzled. What the hell was in Drumheller, besides weird rock formations and dinosaur bones? "What's he doing in Drumheller?"

He didn't answer right away, but I could tell he was going to.

"Drumheller Pen," he finally said, still staring down at the road.

Turned out that in September Sleeve's dad had gotten two years for his part in a hash-oil deal in Leduc. Sleeve and his mom had moved down to Calgary to live with his aunt so that they'd be close enough to visit him sometimes, and this weekend he was getting released on parole.

Sleeve never did. Visit him, I mean.

I know Sleeve seems like kind of a prick sometimes, and he is. He's not one to follow the rules or the proprieties. But believe me, he's *obsessed* about following the law.

Sleeve and I meet up on the easternmost Seventh Avenue LRT platform and head south to grab a beer and a bite before he goes home and I go back to work. He's wearing a silver-grey three-button suit and a diamond-patterned navy bow tie. An occasional affectation of his. He has a purple paisley one too. The cars are all packed so we end up pressed together near one of the doors, hanging onto the same scuffed chrome pole. I'll have to remember to wash my hands when I get home.

The train lurches off. A community-college type with thumping headphones has left his backpack on, and it smacks against my elbow. I edge a little closer to Sleeve.

"Nice tie," I say. Something to say. "Do all the finance nerds get those?"

He smiles but doesn't answer. He just takes one end of the tie between two fingers, pulls slowly until it flops loose, and arranges it so that it dangles down both sides of his well-pressed shirt front.

"The point of the bow tie isn't the bow," he says. "It's the undoing it at the end of the day. The James-Bond-at-the-casino look." He adjusts the ends, making sure one hangs slightly lower than the other. He glances around the car, drops his voice slightly. "Major cool points."

I look around at his LRT cool-points audience. Grey-faced office workers. Zit-faced teens. Middle-aged women with plastic shopping bags. Community college guy, still obliviously smacking me with his backpack with every lurch of the train. I look back at Sleeve's tie. "At your desk after dark with your sleeves rolled up maybe. Or chatting up a cute bridesmaid at midnight in a hotel ballroom. But rush hour on the LRT?"

Sleeve just gives me a smug look up and down.

"Nice shirt," he says.

Sleeve is Slovakian, on both sides. Simple. Straightforward. I envy him that sometimes.

"Auntie Rachel, what *are* we?" I remember asking at some family gathering or other. Dad's older sister. She and I were at the dining room table, building a jigsaw puzzle. I was maybe ten years old. A clipper ship on a stormy sea. Funny the details you remember.

"What do you mean, sweetie?" she asked, completing the left edge, the last piece of grey cloud above the horizon.

I mentioned a couple of guys in my class that year. So-and-so was Irish. So-and-so was Italian. "So what are we?"

I remember her look, though, even though I didn't understand it at the time. Wary. A fraction of a glance toward the kitchen, toward the back yard and Dad. The minefield I was walking her into.

"Well," she said carefully, fitting the flag at the top of the mainsail into place, "your Daddy is French, just like our Daddy was. So that means we're French."

"Oh," I said. "OK." And that was that.

All a kid really wants sometimes is a simple answer.

We pick up Sleeve's car from the commuter lot and drive to a nearby *faux* Irish pub that serves mostly things like pasta and quiche but has an excellent fish and chips special every Friday, which is why we're here. The tables are full so we sit at the bar.

Sleeve doesn't get the whole being-a-composer thing—it's bafflingly impractical to him—but he likes to hear about it, or at least pretends to. So over crisp-fried cod and pints of Harp for him and soda water for me and vinegared skin-on fries, I fill him in on what's not happening with the opera.

The waitress forgets to charge us thirty cents for the side of mayo, and Sleeve's insistence that we pay for it slows us down by almost ten minutes.

I knew from the first month of the music program that I was going to major in composition. Most of the other pianists were performance majors, but I couldn't abide all that god-awful 19th century repertoire.

My composition professor was a florid, homuncular man with a salt-and-pepper moustache and a wart under one eye who claimed to be some sort of distant lateral relative of Anton Bruckner. You wouldn't know it from his style, which tended toward tightly dissonant flute duets or spare serial pieces for pizzicato strings. By second year I had settled into writing bad Philip Glass: banal melodies for soprano or oboe over ear-splitting repetitions of the same chord progression. My prof wanted me to work on counterpoint. It was an uneasy relationship.

One morning I was sitting at a battered piano in one of the practice rooms, trying to work out a three-part fugue in quartal harmony. Nothing quite fit. Then some fourth-year brasshole who was doing the Hummel trumpet concerto with the University Orchestra started warming up in the next room, scattering the few thoughts I had. I gathered my music paper into my satchel and stomped off for a coffee. I was affecting sandals well into the fall in those days, so the stomping was a little floppy.

The Music Department shared Craigie Hall with the Drama Department, which you pretty much had to walk through to get to the little basement coffee bar at the other end of the building. As I stomp-flopped past office doors dotted with wry quotes from Restoration comedies, trying to shake Hummel's viral theme from my head, I noticed a woman ahead of me heading in the same direction. She was wearing a tight blue T-shirt over a colourfully-patterned sarong skirt, her long ginger curls spilling from a co-ordinating batik scarf. I'd seen her last semester in a student production of something by Brecht.

She ended up just ahead of me in the coffee line. We were both peeling lids from little creamers when her backpack brushed my satchel, which slid from my shoulder down to my elbow, which splashed hot coffee onto my exposed feet.

"Oh, God," she said, holding a half-peeled creamer between us like an interrupted offering. Then she tipped it, pouring the cool cream onto my scalded toes. She looked up at me, startled, concerned, and started to laugh.

"I don't know why I just did that," she said.

"I can't say I'm too clear about that either, actually."

"Sorry. I mean, I guess I just thought that the cream would be cool, and the coffee, you know. Hot." She lowered her eyes, shaking her head, smiling in chagrined disbelief.

We sat down on one of the ratty couches on the Drama side. (We musicians usually hung out in a separate area through the doorway by the counter.) She brought napkins over and actually wiped my feet, which were blotching pink by then.

"I've noticed you down here before," she said, looking down at my toes. "Going over to the other side, usually."

"Oh yeah?"

"Yeah. You have a kind of a distinctive look, for a music guy." I bristled a little inside. Here it comes. "Are you, like, Indonesian or something?"

Race, already. Shit.

I let it go. It was nice having this strange woman's fingers in the tender, private spaces between my toes.

"French." Inside joke in honour of Auntie Rachel. When she looked puzzled, I relented. "OK, fine, half Chinese, half assimilated Franco-Albertan." More than half by upbringing I thought, but didn't say.

"Oh. 'Cause your eyes, you know."

It's always the eyes.

No epicanthic fold.

"Yeah," I said. "That's the French part."

Her name was Seana. She was studying acting and dance.

Three weeks later she was my first, though I'm pretty sure I wasn't hers. I remember wrestling the condom on with shaky hands in her parents' basement, not quite willing to believe it was finally happening.

George Michael was playing on the cassette deck—quietly, so that we could hear any footsteps upstairs. Seana's bare shoulders squeaked against the back of their black vinyl couch, and one of my legs hung over onto the floor. I didn't come as soon as I was afraid I would, but it was all still kind of ungainly.

It got better over time.

Sleeve thought she was good for me. Miranda was more sceptical.

"She paints her toenails black and drinks Diet Pepsi for breakfast."

"She's unconventional," I'd reply.

"She won't go out dancing. A dancer, and she won't go out dancing."

"True," I'd say, "but she says to me: 'Suppose there was a club full of pianos, where people with no musical ability could get pissed and just pound away, all at the same time. Would you want to go there?' She has a point."

But Miranda would just shake her head.

By the second term of second year I was in with the drama people through Seana to the point where I was asked to write a few bits of incidental music for a production that she had a supporting role in. My composition prof was against my doing it—he thought it was "an unproductive detour"—so I just left him out of it and fell behind on the stuff that I was actually supposed to be working on.

They needed an overture and six short atmospheric pieces. I created them on the music department's electronic equipment, and then recorded them in order—including the nine sound effects the script called for (thunder, church bells twice, the doorbell twice, the telephone three times, and a window being smashed offstage)—onto reel-to-reel tape for the theatre's aging sound system. It took a lot more of my time than I'd anticipated. Between it and Seana and some part-time hours taking tickets at the Nickle Museum, my course work started seriously slipping.

Part of the deal was that I'd run the recordings from the sound booth during the production, so I was there for the final series of rehearsals. It was amazing. The music took on a whole new depth in the context of the play. The director and I were already in tune, and I got along great with the cast. We'd go for beers after and talk into the night about the nature of art and shit like that. Some of those people are still my friends.

At first Seana seemed happy to be working together, but after a while she became strangely irritable. Finally one night after a half-hearted session on the basement couch it came out.

"You're just so *there* all the time," she said with an affected little pout, tugging the comforter up over her breasts and dramatically folding her arms across it.

I sat up. My damp bum squeaked against the vinyl. "So *where* all the time?"

"Just there. Just *around*, you know? It's not even your department, it's *mine*, it's *my* show, and I'm there busting my ass to be more than just plain old Seana—"

Plain old Seana? Where did that come from?

"Plain old Seana?" I said. "Where did that—"

"Shut up shut up listen to me. Here I am with this, I mean, basically *marginal* role to work with, and the whole time there's my exotic fucking boyfriend"—she lifted her hands, palms forward, fingers spread, framing her face in a parody of naive surprise—" 'oooh, the com*poser*,' always, like, *commandeering* everyone's attention."

My back stiffened. "Your *what* kind of boyfriend?"

"Oh, come on," she said. "Like you don't *know*." Still with the pout, but now also with an almost feral look in her eye. "Like you don't play it *up. Jesus!*"

The muscles in my jaw tightened until my teeth hurt.

I dressed and left without saying a word.

It wasn't actually the end, but it was definitely where the end started. By the time the play ran in May we weren't speaking at all. And I was failing composition. And theory. And I had no idea how I was going to pay for second year. The play went really well, though.

In June there were tanks in Tiananmen Square. I heard about it on the news, but I didn't pay much attention.

And I didn't go back to school in the fall.

Three

Tangshan, July 26, 1976.

At 3:30 a.m. the mine worker is suddenly, inexplicably wide awake. He hears the night-sounds of the other workers: a snore, the creak of a metal bed, footsteps on the floor above. Through the window the odd voice from the current shift's surface staff. He tries to relax back into sleep, but can tell within moments that there's no point.

He gets up quietly and steps outside to urinate. Ten steps to the side of the nearest hut—quicker and simpler than the latrine. As he pulls the front of his trousers down there is a blaze in the sky and the ground under him lifts and falls. Something knocks him down, something else pins his legs. Mad noise, unimaginable, everywhere, like being whipped with chains. The ground lifts and falls again, twisting his legs against whatever has them trapped. His scream is lost in the chaos, choked off by the dust in the air. Through the dust he sees distant arc-lights where a wall should be: The dormitory has become a six-foot heap of bricks and beds and men. Then the heap's surface shifts in the arc-light as the ground lifts and falls again. The mine worker feels leg bone wrench through skin, and loses consciousness.

CBC Radio One is running a piece on Y2K. Louisa and I are rolling the coins from the Montreal Bucket. We've been tossing in our change at the end of each day for three months or so now, and we've probably got enough for about half of a one-way airfare. Still, it surprises me how quickly it's adding up.

"This has been a huge boon to IT companies and consultants," some guy from some American think-tank says. My sense is that most people are getting serious Y2K fatigue by now. Except for Anton, of course. Though I have to say, it still sometimes gives me that chill of things overlooked too. "Converting all of the world's systems by January requires an enormous outlay of tech expertise and an immense amount of code-writing."

Neither of us has ever been to Montreal, and Louisa in particular is very keen. There's some big church that she's seen pictures of that she wants to visit.

Louisa was raised Catholic. She's lapsed now, though not as lapsed as Sleeve. He actually objects to expressions like "fingers crossed" or "touch wood" (which, according to him, originally meant to touch the wood of the cross). I remember Louisa once pointing out to him that all language is essentially metaphor, and that if he wanted to avoid every word or expression the origin of which he didn't agree with philosophically, then he'd end up with a vocabulary of grunts and whistles, and that even some of the whistles might be suspect. She was on such a roll that she went on to point out that the cross, as a symbol, predated Christianity by centuries.

Sleeve responded by grunting.

Then he whistled, as lewdly as he possibly could.

I crimp a plastic cylinder of nickels shut and place it in the Montreal Shoebox with a dozen or so similar cylinders of various sizes. Louise pours another pile of coins onto the table from the bucket and we start fingertipping them into groups by denomination.

"Did you ask that guy at work about camp stoves?" I ask.

She gives me her wry2K look. "Not yet," she says. "I'll get to it. There's plenty of time." Her half-sigh at the end adds *not that it's necessary, of course*, but she's good enough not to articulate that.

I have a decent grouping of dimes, so I start lining them in a dime-sized cylinder, counting them by fives as I go. They nestle neatly into an even, silver column.

"Will all of the necessary code be written in time?" the radio host asks.

"Well," the think-tank guy says, "that's the big question, isn't it?"

Louisa adds a roll of quarters to the shoebox. "You know," she says, "maybe we should spend this on his 'n' hers chemical toilets instead."

Absolutely deadpan.

After I left university I got a job in the office supply warehouse where Dad worked, helping out wherever I was needed. One day I'd be stacking bulk crates of envelopes or ring binders onto high orange industrial shelves, the next I'd be filling commercial orders from the open cartons near the shipping area, and the next I'd be helping the furniture guys deliver filing cabinets and desks. I lost some weight and gained some muscle and was bored out of my fucking mind. I spent a lot of evenings alone in the basement listening to *Dark Side of the Moon* and *The Heart of Saturday Night*.

Filling orders was the most painful. Pick the computer-printed invoice from the tray near the wrapping desk. Gather the listed items from open cartons into a black plastic bin. Two dozen blue pens. One dozen red pens. Three yellow legal pads. One box of standard staples. Deposit the bin at the wrapping desk with the invoice. Check the clock to see how close it is to coffee time. Still two hours. Pick another invoice.

On the other side of a wire-reinforced window near the wrappers was the Order Desk, where the staff who took the phone orders printed off invoices and slid them under the window into the tray. One of the order desk girls, Candace, was almost cartoonishly pretty: extra-large eyes, pixie-cut hair, elfin chin. A tiny zircon nose-ring clung to the edge of her nostril like a shiny booger. After I'd been there about a month, she shared a joint with me in the parked furniture truck during lunch, and a couple of days later she laughingly flashed me her breasts in the back corner of the warehouse behind the credenzas and the crates of steno chairs. One of her nipples pointed slightly inward, as if it was looking over my left shoulder.

I gave her a ride home that night. Her breasts tasted tangy. Some sort of citrus body wash, probably.

Candace shared a two-bedroom duplex with her housemates, Mary and Mary. She had a roughly-framed room in the basement with bare wallboard and a painted concrete floor. It was under Quiet Mary's room, which was good, because there was often quite a lot of mattress noise and soft yelping from Wild Mary's room, especially on the weekends. Candace didn't have much furniture: an unbleached futon on a pine frame, a particle-board wardrobe, a thickly-painted wooden chair. A series of plastic milk crates held her clothes, and another one functioned as a night table. As a space it was barely liveable. For the rest of that summer and most of the fall, though, it was a little corner of erotic heaven.

One Sunday morning around Halloween we were sitting at Candace's kitchen table having toaster waffles and bargain syrup. She was looking at me with this funny smile when Wild Mary and some guy she'd known for about six hours shuffled in all shiny with sweat and looking for coffee. Mary nudged the guy toward the kettle and the jar of instant and then slumped into the chair across from me.

"Hey," Candace said to Mary. She gestured toward me with her head. "Look at this guy."

"Hmmm," Mary said indifferently, finger-combing her damp hair back behind one ear.

Candace gave me that funny smile again. "Isn't he just too cute? Lean. Handsome. He's just so, um … oh, I don't know. What's the word I'm looking for?"

Wild Mary picked up a cold waffle with her fingers and took a bite. "Exotic?"

I stopped chewing.

Candace's face lit up. "Yeah. That's exactly it." She was beaming at me. "Exotic."

I put down my fork.

It wasn't the end. But.

By the end of the month I'd given my notice, and two weeks after that I was gone. Dad lasted until just after the New Year.

According to the display on the phone there have been three calls this week from the 323 area code, but there haven't been any messages. After the second call I looked it up. It's in Los Angeles. As far as I know we don't know anyone there. When the fourth call comes, I'm home.

"Mr. Lavoie?" she asks. She's American, so she gets the name right. *La-voy.*

"Yes?"

"Are you the Jason Lavoie who has a string trio called *Infernal Variations* on a CD on the CBC Records label?" She sounds very perky.

"Yes, that's me."

Someone in L.A. gets CBC recordings?

"Oh, good." She sounds genuinely pleased. It only occurs to me later that the pleasure might have to do with not having to keep looking for the right Jason Lavoie. She gives me her name, and the name of the production company in L.A. that she's with. It's a pretty big name. The company's, I mean. Big as in significant, not as in long.

Someone at a mega-merged media conglomerate's production company in L.A. gets CBC recordings?

"Mm-hmm," I say.

"Mr. Lavoie, I'm calling on behalf of Mr. Ephraim Grant, about your string trio."

I make an effort not to choke.

Prominent action film directors get CBC recordings?

"Mr. Lavoie," the perky woman from L.A. says, "do you have representation?"

Over the next three days I hire a Toronto-based entertainment lawyer, and over the next eight weeks she gets me a decent-sized cheque and a signed promise of more. Maybe not a whole hell of a lot in absolute terms, but in my terms it's all sweet jumpin' Jesus. In exchange, a subsidiary of a subsidiary of the media conglomerate gets certain carefully-defined rights to make use of the 'river of boiling blood' section from Variation Seven of my *Infernal Variations*.[6] The way I understand it, someone in L.A. will now re-record it, and someone will carve a little snippet out of it, and someone will insert that snippet into a scene in which a well-known action star's eyes narrow and then widen just before a truck full of explosives ploughs into the abutment of a bridge.

All because Eph Grant's wife is from Vancouver, and her sister works for the CBC, and he has a habit of idiosyncratically scoring his own films.

"Pack a bag," I say to Louisa.

She can shake loose a four-day weekend.

We're going to Montreal.

In the summer of 1995 — Jesus, nearly five years ago now — I was scoring a production of an original two-act play that a local theatre group called Frozen Elbow was producing at the Pumphouse Theatre. They were people I originally met through Seana. Good actors

---

6. A dark duet in the low registers of the cello and viola supporting a series of irregular, percussive attacks from the violin, in case you're curious.

for the most part, but lousy business people. They folded before the end of their first season. Two of them moved to Toronto and the rest stayed here. You see a couple of their names in dinner theatre ads sometimes. I think one of the others went to law school.

The play was a vaguely postmodern piece about property speculators, millenarian angst, the internment of Japanese-Canadians during World War II, and a young Ukrainian immigrant's abiding love for his grandmother. There were three spots where characters spoke directly to audience, and two brief nude scenes (one involving the grandmother, though in a flashback to when she was nineteen).

That summer I was writing bad Messiaen—mosaics of percussive sound-ideas and my own half-assed transcriptions of birdsong—and throwing around words like *jeremiad* and *chinoiserie*. I stuck to birds that could be found locally, like the European Starling (a simple repetitive motif with a kind of skipping rhythm) or the Loggerhead Shrike (a repeated rising fifth, with the top note tightly clipped).

The borrowed style seemed a little off for the production, even leaving aside the fact that I didn't have Messiaen's orchestral resources. What I had was me on my feeble old synth, trying to strike an impossible balance between too thin and too *Chariots of Fire*, and Miranda on clarinet, struggling heroically with the song of the Warbling Vireo.

To complicate things further Sleeve and Miranda had started dating, which pissed me off. I mean sure, she and I were never going to get together, but Sleeve? That was a bit close to home.

They lasted a little over a year, followed by an awkward period where they moved in slightly different circles for a while, and then gradually they slid back to being friends again. Miranda's good at that. Eighteen months later she married Anton, and in the meantime Sleeve was with whoever he was with at that point, Lexi maybe, or maybe Janice, and that was that.

That Pumphouse summer, though, they were icky close, and I was crabby and alone.

The score for the show fit comfortably on a single reel of tape, which Miranda and I recorded on borrowed equipment in Sleeve's parents' garage. There was a three-and-a-half-minute opening (which ended with the Shrike-call repeating and fading as the curtain rose), a six-minute finale (the same material reworked and extended to cover any curtain calls), and, in between, a half-dozen shorter bits and sound effects.

They ran twelve shows over ten days. Their best crowd was about sixty, which was about three-quarters of what the space could seat. Their worst was the final matinee, a perfect, clear-skied Saturday afternoon when they drew about ten. At each performance I sat in the tech booth and followed a pencil-marked script waiting for my cues.

There was no stage as such, just a small performance space defined by a black curtain at the back and rows of stacking chairs along the front and sides. The windows of the booth were two or three metres up from the last row of seats and maybe five or so from the performers. There were long stretches when my mind could safely wander, and I often found myself scanning the little clusters of people in the audience.

Les, the lighting guy, had a lot more cues to follow than I did, but he found time for his share of audience-gazing too. I'd worked with Les before. Good guy. Probably three hundred pounds, with dark hair, a red biker moustache, and a crushed straw cowboy hat that he wore indoors and out, all year long. About a half-hour in on closing night he gestured toward a small group of young women over to the left.

"That one keeps looking up here."

"Which one?" I peered down into the gallery. There was a significant scene change before my next cue, so I could afford to relax my attention a little.

"Blonde."

"Big glasses?"

"Yeah."

She was peering at her program in the dark. Then her head turned and she was looking straight into the booth.

I drew back.

Sleeve and Miranda were there that night, so at intermission I scrambled down to find them and get a quick coffee. The stairs from the booth led down through a closed door to a short set of steps by the theatre entrance. I took the short set too quickly, slipped on the bottom step, and barely caught my balance against the exposed brick wall.

I looked up and saw the woman with the big glasses on her way out of the theatre, looking right at me.

I laughed to myself and shook my head. Figures.

Sleeve and Miranda were entwined at the back of the beverage line, each with a hand in the other's back pocket. I waved as I walked over to join them, mostly just to see how they'd manage to wave back. Miranda used her free hand. Sleeve just nodded.

"So," I asked, "how does it all fit?" Up until now Miranda had only known the music in the abstract. She hadn't heard it in the context of the play. Sleeve hadn't heard it at all.

"Pretty well," she said. "The intro was nice, and the jagged bit when the young man thinks the woman in the front row is his grandmother nicely undercut the unintended humour." She paused and frowned slightly. "Not so sure about the starling song when the working poor are being evicted, though."

"Yeah, my inner Messiaen may have slipped away from the service of the narrative a little there."

"I don't know what the fuck you two are talking about," Sleeve said, "but the redhead sure has nice snibs for a grandma."

Miranda pulled her hand out of his pocket and lightly slapped the back of his head.

Sleeve nodded at me gravely. "I may have deserved that," he said.

"You did," Miranda said, pulling him closer and smiling up at him. Then they actually leaned together and rubbed noses.

"Okay," I said, "I'm going to look away now so I don't soil your evening-out clothes with my puke."

Sleeve shook his head.

"Weak stomach, man. It'll be your downfall."

Miranda and I got coffees. Sleeve got a local draft, and paid for all of us.

"Cheers man," I said, clinking my Styrofoam cup against his plastic glass. "Thanks for the coffee."

"No prob. Thanks for the unbearable tunes."

"Just doin' my job."

I pushed off through the crowd, and as I looked back to make sure Miranda and Sleeve were following, I saw Big Glasses at the counter ordering a glass of wine. She couldn't have been more than a couple of people behind us in the line. I wondered if she'd heard any of our conversation.

Had I said anything totally embarrassing? My mind crawled back over the conversation as the three of us made our way past a wall of little brass donor-recognition plaques and down some stairs to a less crowded spot near some vending machines. No, I was probably fine. A little pretentious maybe, but the embarrassing bits had probably all been Sleeve. A normal night out.

Miranda and I talked about the sound quality for a bit, while she periodically rested her head on Sleeve's chest and he surreptitiously scoped out the room's cleavage supply. Soon the crowd started to thin. I looked at my watch and gulped the last of my coffee. "Gotta get back up." I looked at Sleeve. "Snib alert in scene two, by the way."

And I scampered away before Miranda could slap my head.

"The blonde with the glasses is looking up here again," Les said during the scene where the millenarians strip off their clothes as a gratuitous symbol of the purity of the end times. Why he was watching the crowd instead of the stage at that point I have never understood. "I think she's looking at you."

"Yeah. She saw me nearly take a header on the stairs at intermission."

"Wave to her."

"I don't think so."

She turned to one of her friends and pointed to something on her program. They both looked up. Les tipped his cowboy hat to them, and they quickly looked away.

I was waiting for Sleeve and Miranda near the now-closed bar while they went to the washroom. Not to the *same* washroom, I hoped, or I could be waiting for a while. I'd picked up the brochure for the rest of Frozen Elbow's season, and noticed with interest that they were doing *Krapp's Last Tape* in February. I was wondering if they'd ask me to do the sound design[7] when a voice from behind startled me.

"Did you write the music?" the voice asked.

I twitched, then looked around. It was Big Glasses. By herself.

"Um, yes. Yes I did."

She nodded. "It was really good."

"Thanks." I nodded back. I'm not sure why. "That's nice to hear."

There was a slightly-too-long pause while each of us reached for something to say. She got there first.

"Can I ask you something that might sound stupid?"

I nodded. I seemed to be doing a lot of that. "Sure. I guess."

"Was some of it based on birdsong?"

I brightened. "Yeah, in a few spots. Thanks for noticing." I was surprised that she could tell. "How could you tell?" I asked.

It turned out that she had a four-CD box set of Messiaen's opera *Saint François d'Assise*—which is absolutely *crawling* with

---

7. They didn't.

birdsong—that a wiccan co-worker of hers had given to her for its mystical energy.

Her name was Louisa. She worked for a marketing firm downtown called Brownspring Scunthorpe, conducting focus groups and then crunching the data that came out of them. She liked CFL football and she owned her own curling broom. She asked me if I wanted to get a glass of wine or something somewhere.

"What happened to your friends?"

She looked around, as if she'd just noticed that they were gone. "Oh, they were heading to some cowboy bar on Macleod Trail. I told them to go without me. Not my thing." She looked around again. "What about *your* friends?"

The area near the washrooms was empty and quiet.

"I think they've forgotten about me. Where would you like to go?"

She knew a place not far away that wasn't too crowded or too expensive. We got into our cars and I followed her along the little two-lane access road under Crowchild Trail and out onto Ninth. We took 8th Street south to 17th Avenue and found adjacent parking spaces in a backstreet lot.

The bar was a bare-brick loft with heavy pine tables and light Okanagan wines. I got a of glass of Shiraz for her and a Coke for me and we settled into a corner table by the window.

"You didn't want wine?" she asked.

"I don't drink."

She didn't ask why. I liked that.

I took a sip of my Coke and wiped the rim of the glass with my napkin. "So," I said. "Why are we here?"

"I thought we'd covered that. It's a nice place to get a drink."

"No, I mean why me? I'm a complete stranger."

She looked down at the table with a shy *why are you asking me this?* smile. "I don't know," she said. "You seemed nice. I liked your music."

I folded the napkin in half with the Coke stain inside and lined it up with the edge of the table. "I seemed nice? Through the tech booth window, from across the room?"

"We talked, remember?"

"Well yes, that's true, we did." I paused. "*After* you ditched your friends."

She dropped her chin, flushing slightly, and fiddled with a clunky red ring on one thumb. Stalling, while she decided whether or not to say something. Then, eyes still on the ring, she spoke again.

"You laughed at yourself."

"Hmm?"

She lifted her eyes, smiled. "When you stumbled. Coming down from the booth, at intermission. You laughed at yourself. It was sweet."

After the drinks there was a soft kiss goodnight and an exchange of phone numbers, and after the movie the following weekend there was some breathless groping in my car in front of her building, and after the chamber concert the weekend after that she came up to my apartment and we fucked until four and slept until noon and had toast and coffee on my balcony.

"Hard! Hard, darn it!"

Teresa's voice echoed off the high, arched ceiling. My sister can get quite worked up about curling, but not to the point of profanity.

Teresa is a long-legged six footer who dreams of the anonymity of five-eight. She spent most of high school fending off desperate coaches' entreaties to join the basketball team or the volleyball team or to go out for track *just for this season Terry, just until we build up a little more depth in the distance events.*

She hates being called Terry.

The state of her denial during her grade nine growth spurt had extended to asking our bald, baffled GP if it was possible to have any vertebrae surgically removed, which had led to a couple of inconclusive years of emotional therapy. The last thing she was interested in was any sport that called attention to her height. So she curled.

Sliding knee-to-chest, low to the ice during the release or hunched over the broom as she swept, the brave or ill-informed might at worst say that she looked *long*, but damn sure no-one would have to look up to meet her eye.

She had a rink in a local league—herself, a bank guy who Sleeve also knew and a couple of dentists—and I was an alternate. I'd agreed earlier in the week to fill in that Saturday after Bob the dentist can-celled because his wife was taking him to the Banff Springs Hotel for their anniversary weekend. Then on the Friday Rick the dentist's kid came home from her day care with lice and he had to spend the weekend shaving their heads and boiling their furniture, or what-ever the hell you do when your kid has lice, and since it was un-thinkable that Teresa's rink default and I was the only alternate, I took a flyer and asked Louisa if she was interested. We'd been togeth-er for a couple of months by then, and she *did* have her own broom.

My sweeping was apparently not hard enough, as Kamal the bank guy's rock curled too far too soon and ended up essentially useless as the guard that it was meant to be. As I slid back down the ice I heard Teresa viciously mutter *son of a biscuit*. I waved to Ter-esa's husband Ed in the snack bar as our opponent readied his second shot.

Teresa and Ed are the kind of folks who hand-dig their dande-lions and have their disposable diapers recycled. He's a mid-level lawyer in a mid-level oil and gas law firm, and she manages two locations of a strip-mall hair salon with a name that puns on sheer/shear or main/mane. (I always forget which.) They're active in Ro-tary and the local Y and the Chinese United Church.

Ed was sitting on a varnished plywood chair at a *faux* leather folding table, pointing us out to their son Bobby—who was prob-ably four or five months old at the time—through the scratched Plexiglas window. I could practically hear him narrating every sound and colour and glint of light to the poor overstimulated loaf. Ed is all about the teachable moments. Louisa slid up beside me and patted my bum, and Ed made a theatrical show of covering Bobby's eyes.

The other guy's shot went nowhere, and Kamal was back up. I nudged Louisa and gestured toward Ed with my broom handle. "See Bobby," I said in a singsong-y voice, "there's *Mommy* down there in the *red* jacket. She's the *skip*, which means she's the boss. She's using her *broom* to tell Uncle *Kamal* where she wants his *rock* to go. Uncle *Kamal* is in the *green* jacket."

"Shhhhh," Louisa said, half-snickering and looking quickly toward Teresa. She slapped my shoulder with a mittened hand. "Just get ready."

Kamal let go, and on Teresa's sharp command Louisa and I bore down again with our brooms (I favoured the satisfying *thwack thwack* of the old corn broom to the weeny scrubbing with the apparently-more-effective push broom that the rest of them were using—always an issue for Teresa) in a vain effort to keep Kamal's final rock close to centre in front of the twelve-foot ring.

When it came to rest—again too far left to be any use as a guard—Teresa grimaced and spun away toward the scoreboard. We were tied four all after nine ends, and the other rink—two women and two men from a rival dental practice—were poised to take two points in this, the final end. Teresa had been trying to get Kamal to set up a guard for Louisa to draw in behind, ideally somewhere inside the four-foot ring where the two rival rocks presently sat.

Louisa and I glided back down the ice, she to set up for her first rock and me to get ready to sweep again. One of the rival dentists was already in the hack, sliding his rock back and forth, his sweepers poised to go.

"So we've got some family getting together to watch the Calgary-Regina game tonight," I said to Louisa as we slid. "Chips and beer, probably order some pizza. You want to come?"

It was the first time I'd suggested getting together with my family. She hesitated, a little blindsided.

"You're not Rider fans, are you?" she finally asked with a slight eyebrow-raise.

"A couple of my cousins are, but only one of them will be there. Is that a deal breaker?"

She smiled as she turned to watch the rival rock pass us on its way to run clear through the house without effect. "Can we stop at my place to change first? I don't want to stay in these socks all evening."

And then she was off to the hack to set up for her shot.

Teresa tapped a spot just to the left of the button, where she wanted Louisa to place her rock. I thought she was being optimistic —Louisa probably didn't have room to get past the nearer of the rival rocks without nudging it into an even better position. As it turned out that didn't matter. She gave her rock way too much weight, overcompensating for the late-game slowness of the ice. It was probably the same thing that the rival dentist had just done, and to the same effect: Her rock sailed right through the house. Kamal and I just stood and watched. It was clear from the moment Louisa let go that there was no need to sweep.

Louisa, still stretched out along the ice, hung her head. Teresa just scowled.

I slid over to Louisa as she got up. "It ain't over," I said.

"Don't bet on it."

The rival dentist threw his final rock. Its edge caught a particularly slow patch of ice just over the hog line and, despite the intense scrubbing of his sweepers, it lost quite a lot of spin. Instead of curling in to guard their shot rock it nudged it even closer to the button —in better scoring position, but now unguarded.

Teresa smiled.

Louisa redeemed herself by almost managing a double take-out, nudging the dentists' shot rock to the back of the twelve-foot and clearing their other one out altogether. Their skip put one just left of centre in the eight-foot, which Teresa then drew in behind for shot rock, setting us all bouncing and high-fiving and Ed dancing Bobby on his knees behind the Plexiglas until the dentists' skip tapped Teresa's rock back to the eight-foot and stuck almost on the button.

Teresa's last rock should have been an easy take-out, but somehow she misread the ice and her rock hardly curled at all and she barely brushed the dentists' winning rock before sailing out the other end of the house.

"Drat!" echoed off of the rafters, drawing puzzled glances from the neighbouring rinks.

"Good game anyhow," Ed said with a grin as he shouldered through the flimsy swinging door, his baby locked solidly in both arms. He hovered well back from the ice as he waited for my sister to finish shaking hands with the dentists, no doubt picturing his foot rocketing sideways on the pebbled white surface, flinging Bobby out of his grasp and into a life of paraplegia.

"Louisa is coming to watch the ball game today," I said.

Ed's eyebrows went up. "Really? Since when?"

"Since just now."

Ed nodded. "All right," he said.

There was always a family Grey Cup party when I was growing up. I remember one year in particular when it was at Uncle Derrick and Auntie Rachel's, which was the worst possible place other than Uncle Mark's. Uncle Derrick belonged to a fundamentalist church called the Brethren of Christ Crucified, a venomous Idaho- or Montana-based sect of the sort of Christians who would happily drive the needle through the eye of the camel. Auntie Rachel followed along to the BCC to keep the peace, though her natural sympathies were, I think, secretly Catholic. "Secretly" because Uncle Derrick never outgrew his formative protestant-school contempt for popery.

That's what makes the memory of that Grey Cup day particularly sharp. It would have been a shock to hear anyone advise

Mama to leave my father, but to hear it from Auntie Rachel—who had an "Abortion Kills Children" bumper-sticker on her sewing basket and said grace over her morning tea—was unimaginable.

Edmonton was ahead of Hamilton 31 to 4 when the gun signalled half time, rousing everyone (meaning mostly the men and the kids) from their spots on the couch and the floor. My cousin Neil—high on western pride I, assume—gave me a celebratory kick on his way to the kitchen for another root beer.

It was Neil's late-in-life arrival after a series of miscarriages that brought Uncle Derrick to the church, though not to the specific church Auntie Rachel credited with the miracle. I can't imagine what it took to get Uncle Derrick to take her to that miracle-church in Montreal. He certainly wouldn't have gone with her to the actual shrine. He has always credited Jesus alone with granting him a son, fiercely rejecting the notion that some dead priest or his pointy-hatted Pope may have had a role. When Uncle Derrick reached out to the church in his gratitude, he made sure to reach for one more in line with his own temperament.

I was looking for a place to hide out and read the new Spider-man I'd brought when I heard Auntie Rachel's voice in one of the back bedrooms. From the hallway shadows I saw her looking at a palm-sized bruise on Mama's forearm.

"You can't keep putting up with this," she said as she rolled down and rebuttoned Mama's sleeve. "How can you possibly stay?"

Mama cradled her arm and winced.

"I wouldn't give the bastard the satisfaction."

I last saw Derrick and Rachel three Easters ago along with a scattering of other relatives at their downsized condo. They still had crosses in every room. While the women cooked, Uncle Derrick sat in his armchair reading the obits and muttering: "Older. Younger. Younger. Older. Older." After dinner Auntie Rachel hummed hymns to herself and did crosswords from a book.

Neil has been on meds for schizophrenia since he was fifteen.

One time before they got him stabilized he accused me of trying to steal his penis.

Uncle Derrick's God has some dark sense of humour.

The snack bar at the curling rink was licensed, and we had a drink there with Teresa and Ed before heading to their place to watch the game. After a little while Bobby went mercifully to sleep in his stroller, and Ed bundled Teresa's gear out to the car.

"If there'd been just a little less bite to the ice ..." I said, but Teresa waved me off as she downed the last swallow of white wine from her plastic cup.

"Never mind," she said, tossing the glass into a green garbage bin. "It's done." She looked at her watch. "Oh jeepers, I'd better go. We still have to pick up the pop." She stood up. "You coming?"

I tilted my head toward my Coke and Louisa's half-full rum cooler. "Couple of minutes yet. We'll see you there, though."

Teresa's eyes brightened. "You're coming too, Louisa? Great. Six-thirty." And off she went with the stroller, ducking slightly as she passed through the door.

Louisa took a sip of cooler and stared at my eyes over the rim of the plastic cup. A funny stare. She put the cup down. "You know," she said, "you look so. Um." She angled her head a little, frowning slightly. "Oh, what's the right word?"

Here it comes, I thought. *Fuck*.

Just when things seemed to be going well, too.

"Exotic," I said flatly. Resigned rather than annoyed.

It was probably inevitable. Not the end, but.

Plus it was sure going to fuck up football night.

Louisa drew back and scowled in surprise. "No-oo," she said, a bewildered look in her eyes. "I was going to say something like 're-laxed' or 'contented,' which is something I don't get to see in you very often."

I just sat there.

She shook her head, laughing. "Exotic? *Please.* Look around you." She made a sweeping arm gesture, taking in the sheets of ice through the plastic windows, the snack bar, the scabby tables and chairs. "We've just been curling. *Curling,* Jason. And now we're about to go out to the suburbs to watch CFL football and eat ripple chips and drink Canadian beer." She put her hand on my arm and gave me an indulgent smile. "I'm sorry, Jason. You're sweet, and hot, but you're about as far from exotic as it gets."

My heart did a joyful tap-dance.

We moved in together three weeks later.

Four

WE ARRIVE IN MONTREAL IN THE MIDDLE OF THE AFTERNOON——
bagged from the flight but determined not to waste any time—and
check into our B & B near Carré Saint-Louis. The room is small
and poorly laid out, with the wardrobe behind the door, the shower
half-barricaded by the toilet, and the lone east-facing window directly above the head of the narrow bed.

It's perfect.

The morning sun might be a problem, though. The curtains are
very thin.

We crowd our toiletries onto the tiny shelf over the bathroom
sink and unpack our clothes. Louisa, who doesn't overpack the way
I do, finishes first and starts to help with mine.

"What's wrong?" Louisa asks.

"What?"

"You rehung that shirt I just hung there."

I stop to notice. "Oh. Sorry."

"It doesn't matter. I just wondered why you did it."

I look into the wardrobe. "It was the wrong way around."

"Wrong way around? What way?" She pushes around my shoulder and peers in. "Oh my God!" she says, laughing. "Your shirts all
face the same direction!"

"Yeah? So?"

After all, here I am, paying for *her* dream trip …

She turns to me, frames my face in her hands and kisses me, smiling. "Nothing. Nothing at all. It's cute."

A little later, as I'm putting my shoes on, she goes back to the wardrobe for her sweater and laughs again. "Your hangers all hook the same direction too!"

"But that just makes sense. It's easier to hook them outside in than inside out."

She bends to kiss my cheek. "Yes, dear."

We head back out on foot to browse the shops along rue Saint-Denis. Louisa buys a gauzy amber scarf and drapes it over her shoulders. We have *café au lait* on a tiny patio a few steps below sidewalk level. Along a single block of street-vendors' tables we try on eight hats and a dozen pairs of sunglasses, and I buy two used Jacques Brel CDs for ten bucks each. At sunset we find a candle-lit restaurant in Old Montreal and have poached sole and *frites* under a Cinzano umbrella on the terrace.

As I wipe the last of the thick, slightly sharp sauce from my plate with bits of baguette, Louisa clears a space on her side of the table and brings out the guidebooks. "So," she says, flipping one open to a map with dime-sized icons for the local attractions and bright colourful lines for the main roads and subway routes, "what do you most want to see here?"

"Mmmmm," I say as my lips close around the last fragment of bread.

Louisa looks up, smiling. "The Mornay?" she asks.

She's lost me. I crane my neck to see the map. "I guess so. Where is it?" I haven't done much prep for this trip compared to Louisa.

She gives me a blank *are you fucking with me* look, then an amused smirk once she realizes that I'm not. "No, you half-wit. That erotic moan of yours just now. The Mornay sauce?"

Oh.

Her eyes look amazing in candlelight when she laughs.

After dinner we go to a small jazz club with exposed brick walls and inoffensive watercolours. It's full but not crowded—genteel couples on genteel dates. The host seats us at a table with four other people. We all nod and mumble for a moment and then politely ignore one another.

The band—trombone backed by piano trio—is in the middle of a quirky arrangement of something by Ellington that I can't quite name. The bass player looks like a palsied actuary, with his rimless bifocals and quivering head-bobs. The pianist crouches over his keyboard like Schroeder from Charlie Brown.

They're good, though.

The set goes fast. It ranges from Monk to Metheny, with a few pretty interesting originals, all with a kind of reined-in energy that keeps threatening to slip out of control. Even on the standards there are enough adventurous harmonies to keep it interesting, and every so often they let go of fixed rhythm altogether and just soar. They round off the set with a screaming-hot Coltrane tune, and I look over at Louisa in dizzy satisfaction.

Her forehead is clenched.

She's not enjoying it.

I wave at the server for another white wine and another Coke, and ask Louisa what the problem is.

"Nothing. It's fine."

"Your forehead is clenched."

She frowns a little. "I'm getting a bit of a headache, actually."

Oh.

Shit.

"Oh," I say. I don't say the 'shit' part.

"It's not the music?"

There's a pause. "No. It's fine."

Fine. Now *there's* a blurb for the CD jacket.

Funny thing, perception. I'd happily stay until the drummer packed the last cymbal into the back of his hatchback and headed off home to wherever jazz drummers live in Montreal. To Louisa it's an emerging headache.

"Do you have anything for it?"

She rubs her forehead. "No."

"Here." I dig out the flat pill case that I always carry. "Have an Advil." There are two of them, along with two antacids and two antihistamines. She takes one and swallows it dry. I'll replace it when we get back to the B & B.

The server angles around our tablemates and sets down Louisa's fresh wine and my Coke. I hand him some bills and wave off the change. "Listen," I say over the ambient din. "We have to finish these drinks anyhow. What if we just stay until around the middle of the next set? Is that okay?"

Another pause, then: "Fine."

A Canadian compromise that essentially ends up pissing us both off. It's funny how much less you enjoy something when you know that the person with you is just enduring it.

Three songs into the next set we cab it back to the B & B in cool silence, and by the time I finish washing my face and brushing my teeth she's curled away from me in the bed, the quilt pulled up over her hunched shoulders to her ear. I crawl in beside her. "How's your head?"

"Hmmm hmm," she murmurs into the bedding.

Might mean okay. Might mean leave me alone.

Might mean both.

I turn off the bedside lamp and stare at the ceiling cracks in the shadowy light from the street until I fall asleep.

Breakfast is served in a small, sunny room with frilly white curtains and plasticized tablecloths. There's a sideboard with croissants, bagels and whole grain breads, plus a large basket of fresh fruit and a smaller one with little packets of butter, cream cheese and jam.

One of the owners, a quiet thirtyish woman in an unlikely floral housedress, brings us a chrome carafe of strong coffee and two bowls of berries. Louisa pours the coffee while I toast two bagels, and we settle in at our table.

"Why do you do that?" she asks through a mouthful of berries. We seem to be more or less recovered from last night, as far as I can tell.

"Do what?"

"That thing with the packet of jam. Making that diagonal line with your knife?"

I look down to where I have, as I always do, divided my jam corner to corner. "You've never noticed that?"

"Don't think so."

I slide the knife under one of the jam triangles and lift it from the packet. "It's so I get the same amount on each half of the bagel. Or each piece of toast."

She looks at me oddly.

"What?" I say. "If you divide it side to side it won't necessarily be even."

And her smile in the morning sun lights up the little room.

"You're just so adorable."

Yeah, I guess we're recovered.

After breakfast we get back out into the city, and Louisa opens the map to check for Metro stops.

"Why don't we just walk?"

"You want to walk to the Oratory."

"How hard can it be?" I tap the map. "It's just behind this bump in the middle of the city that they have the nerve to call a mountain."

Louisa shrugs and smiles. "Fine with me."

We head down Avenue des Pins to the rutted road that winds through the forest up the side of Mount Royal. Louisa walks briskly, arms swinging. After a couple of switchbacks I'm breathing a little heavily and starting to lose ground. She looks back and smiles. "There isn't a problem, is there? It's just a little bump in the middle of the city."

"Still not a mountain." It takes some effort to get the words out without gasping, but I do.

I kind of have to.

By the time I reach the open park at the top my heart is hammering in my ears and I've lost sight of Louisa. I find her on a bench by a small lake, sipping bottled water. I sit next to her, suppressing a groan. She hands me the bottle and I tip it back until it's empty.

"Fine," I say. "You've made your point."

"I didn't say it." She slaps my knee and bounces up from the bench. "Come on."

I grunt to my feet and follow her.

At the far side of the park, across a roadway, is a large cemetery, and as we cross toward it I catch my first sight of the Oratory. We steer along the lanes between the graves, heading downward now, to where the land flattens and opens out. We pass through the cemetery gates, cross a major intersection, and follow a gently rising street to the base of the Oratory grounds. As we come around the low-rise buildings that surround it I see it properly for the first time.

It stuns me.

The terraced grounds are enormous, but the Oratory dominates them. It must be a hundred metres tall from its limestone façade to the top of its massive green dome, and about the same wide, not including outbuildings. It's all massive, but it's the dome that hits you. I've noticed it from a distance more than once in the short time we've been here, but I haven't really *seen* it until now. Its scale is so far beyond what I associate with Canada's religious architecture that I'm dumbstruck. It's taller, broader, more ornate. More *committed*. Knox United on Sixth Avenue, which I've always kind of liked, suddenly seems piddling by comparison. It's a paradigm lurch, like finding an NHL team in Moose Jaw or a *premier cru* Bordeaux at Burger King.

"Sweet Jesus," I say.

"That's kind of the idea," Louisa replies.

Three flights of concrete steps rise across the terraced lawns from the parking lot to the church. A separate lane of whitewashed wooden steps runs up the middle of them, marked off with railings and posted with signs. "*Réservé aux pèlerins qui montent à genoux,*" I read aloud. "What does that mean? Reserved for what?"

Louisa shakes her head and chuckles. "You're anglo-assimilated all right. 'For pilgrims who go up on their knees.' See?" She gestures toward the upper flights, where three people are kneeling on the white-washed boards, each at a different level of ascent, each unmoving. One of them advances a single step. We pass them as we climb on the flanking concrete: two older women and a young man, all soberly dressed, all intently clutching rosaries. It's like something out of the Middle Ages.

"I don't get it," I say once we've passed out of earshot.

"Of course you don't," Louisa says. "You're not a pilgrim. You're a tourist."

We pick up guide books and follow the directions to a high-ceilinged room lit by floor-mounted candelabra and ranks of votive candles in tiny red and green glass cups. The chapel walls are hung with dozens—maybe hundreds—of age-darkened crutches and canes and leg braces with hardened leather straps. Relics of pilgrims who came for a cure and apparently left satisfied.

It hits me. "This must be where Auntie Rachel came."

"Auntie Rachel?"

"Uncle Derrick's wife. She talked him into coming to some shrine in Quebec after she'd had a bunch of miscarriages. A year or so later my cousin Neil was born."

"Is Neil the prick who sandbagged you in the garage that time?"

"No, that's Danny. Who's actually not such a prick any more. Anyhow, that's why Derrick and Rachel are such born-agains. God gave them a son."

"I didn't know your family was Catholic."

"Oh, we're not. And certainly not them, though Auntie Rachel probably would be if she could get away with it. They're gun-toting Montana fundamentalists. As far as Uncle Derrick is concerned the Catholics are a deviant cult."

"But they came to a Catholic shrine for help."

"Hey, don't ask me. I think Auntie Rachel heard about it from some neighbour woman and she was desperate. The fundamentalist thing came later, after God came through with Neil."

We walk through the chapel holding hands. *Bas reliefs* on the walls show Saint Joseph in a variety of roles. "So who was this Joseph, some early Canadian priest?"

Louisa stares at me. "Seriously?"

"What? I'm not Catholic. How should I know?"

"Joseph? Jesus' *father*?"

"I thought God was Jesus' father."

"Fine, *step*father. And probably the most understanding husband *ever*."

Each *bas relief* represents a different aspect of Jesus' sainted stepdad. The panels are captioned in French, but I read the translations from the guidebook as we pass. Model for Workers. Terror of Demons.

"Guardian of Virgins?" I put an arm around Louisa. "Nothing for you here, big guy," I say to the panel, and Louisa twists away and smacks me. "Patron of the Dying. Consoler of the Afflicted. Support of Families. He's one busy guy."

"*And* the perfect dad," Louisa says.

We carry on past the tomb of the Oratory's founder, Brother André, and look in quietly on a room called the Crypt Church where a well-attended Mass is going on.

Up a long escalator a kind of lobby with a gift shop opens onto a terrace. I buy a glow-in-the-dark dashboard Jesus, just for giggles. As Louisa wanders over to a stack of shrink-wrapped boxes on a cloth-covered table, I go out onto the terrace. The view is wonderful. Not much to see — houses and apartments and trees — but there's something about the vantage. Louisa joins me and we take pictures of each other with Montreal in the background.

Up another flight of stairs we find a vault-like cabinet with Brother André's actual heart on display in a glass reliquary.

"So this is the magic bit that gives people their legs back?" I ask Louisa.

"And their fertility, apparently."

Another escalator takes us up to the Basilica, inside the dome. The interior is even more striking than the exterior, if that's possible. It must seat a couple of thousand people, though there are only maybe a dozen at the moment, and the pillars and draperies seem to rise to — well, to heaven, I suppose is the point. There's a lot of sculpture — a towering crucifix, elongated modernist apostles, *bas reliefs* of what the guide book says are the stations of the cross — and yet the space is so huge it's still strikingly austere. As a bonus, the organist is practicing. Sounds like one of Bach's chorale preludes. *O Lamm Gottes unschuldig*, maybe.

We sit and listen. After a while Louisa wanders around and looks at the art some more, but I just keep sitting and listening.

I could sit here forever.

That night we have Greek food at a bring-your-own-wine restaurant on Prince Arthur. Louisa enjoys her half-bottle of local *Seyval Blanc* so much that between the salad and the souvlaki I slip to the *depanneur* next door for another to take back to our room. After coffee and dessert we walk back to the hotel arm in arm, finding everything glorious along the way. We climb contentedly into bed and talk softly in the dark about parks and dinky mountains and the stillness of churches. Curled into Louisa's shoulder I drift to sleep and dream about Joseph, the patron saint of good dads.

In the morning we wake within moments of each other, just before dawn, each with the same gentle hunger. We shift onto our knees with Louisa's elbows on the windowsill and make quiet rear-entry love as we watch the sun rise.

The east-facing window isn't such a problem after all.

We doze together a little afterward, then go down to breakfast, where Louisa smirks again at my diagonal jam-division. This morning the fruit bowl is only sliced banana and melon balls, but the pastry tray includes fresh *brioche*.

After breakfast we take the metro to Pie IX station, then wander—Louisa peering at the signs as we go—toward what's apparently some sort of surprise. "There it is," Louisa says as we arrive at a set of traffic lights.

I don't see it. Then I do.

"The botanical garden? This is the surprise? Flowers?"

"You'll see," she says, smiling, grabbing my sleeve. The light changes and we cross, Louisa skipping like a kid, swinging my arm. "You'll see-ee," she sings. My chest tingles with reflected delight. I lift her in a spinning hug in the middle of the street, and she laughs into my eyes. A horn toots. We run to the other side as traffic stirs behind us.

Louisa pays our way in and walks me past roses roses roses bench roses roses trellis roses roses until finally she stops by a knobbly rock perched on another knobbly rock. She turns to face me, smiling.

"This is it? Rocks?"

"This is where it *starts*."

A flat stone path through the trees to the right opens to a tile-topped white wall, with a row of small ornate windows and a large canopied gate. The canopy's pillars and beams are lacquered a rich red-brown, its steps flanked by squat stone animals. Dragons or lions maybe. The shift from roses roses roses rocks knocks me still.

"It's ... is it Chinese?"

Louisa nods, grinning. "A whole formal garden. Come on."

The gate opens into a walled courtyard. Three more knobbly rocks in a tableau opposite the gate. The wall behind them stretches to the left and humps up over a circular opening tall enough to walk through. At the far end is a *bas relief* of long-necked birds flying over water, past clouds petalled like roses.

"It's beautiful," I say.

"It's through there, actually," Louisa says, pointing toward the circular gate.

She has a pamphlet, which she occasionally refers to. "The wall protects the garden. The gate is the only way in. It's called a moon gate. Because it's round, I guess."

"Protect it from what?"

She shrugs. "I don't know. In-*vaaaaa*-ders," she says in a mock-ominous voice, and laughs.

The garden covers a lot of ground. Paths wind past arrangements of gnarled white rocks, across small bridges, between compact groves of trees. We follow them, stop, consult the pamphlet, carry on. Every element seems to have a meaning, though none of it is apparent to me. Soon I'm overwhelmed trying to keep up.

And Louisa has foreseen that.

She pulls a thermos of green tea and two porcelain cups from her bag and leads me to a small hexagonal structure the pamphlet tells us is called the Pavilion of Infinite Pleasantness. It's essentially just six red-brown pillars supporting a sharply upswept tile roof, but its proportions are soothing and it's a nice place to sit.

"Thoughts?" She looks a little concerned. My agitation must show.

"I don't know. It ... it's beautiful. But I think I keep expecting it to, I don't know. Speak to something in me."

"And it isn't?"

I shake my head and sip my tea. "Nope."

"Why would it? You thinking you should have some sort of race memory?"

"Of course not."

"So you're thinking this is where all that Chinese culture that you had growing up should kick in, then?" She says it lightly, but it hits me in the gut like an elbow and I double over, spilling my tea. "Oh my God, Jason, what's the matter?" She's on me in an instant, arm around my shoulders, cheek nuzzling the back of my slumped head. And I can't even answer. Can't articulate the enormity of this acre of landscaped meaning that's so meaningless to me.

"That rotten bastard," I finally say, throat tight. Then there are no more words. Just long, shaking sobs.

After a while Louisa pours me more tea and holds me in the Pavilion of Infinite Pleasantness while I drink it silently. She closes the guide book and puts it away.

"Baby steps," she says. "You aren't going to catch up all in one day." She leads me out of the garden and back to the hotel and undresses me and tucks me into our bed and sits with me until I sleep.

God I love this woman.

The week goes too fast. We drink a lot of coffee on a lot of patios, and shop for clothes on Sainte-Catherine, and sleep late and make quiet love in the afternoon and go back to the Oratory twice just to sit in the Basilica under the dome. On our last morning I go to the Chinese garden on my own and try to take it in without thinking about it until it stops making me sad, and after a while it almost works.

Over our last dinner, on a patio in Old Montreal, we give each other little gifts to remember the trip by. We'd agreed they should be tacky, so I give her the glow-in-the-dark dashboard Jesus from the gift shop at the Oratory. Her gift turns out not to be tacky at all, though I guess she must have thought it was when she bought it. It's a model kit—an assortment of punch-out pieces of balsa wood that slot together on a hardwood base into a skeletal Oratory about nine inches high. It's all there, and quite ornate—the base, the stairs, the terrace, the dome.

"Awesome," I say.

"Mine too." She makes her glow-in-the-dark Jesus do a little dance on the table.

And the next day it's cabs and airports and laundry, and pretty soon I'm back opening the store like it never happened at all.

PART II

Five

A COUPLE OF WEEKS AFTER WE GET BACK TERESA AND ED HAVE a barbecue.

Ed's always upgrading his audio equipment and adding to his CD collection. I see them maybe three or four times a year, and there's always some new tweak to show me, or some new Boccherini or Bill Evans to listen to.

Their house is in one of the newer large-lot developments that sprawl across the rangelands on what used to be the south edge of town. They have a driveway that runs clear to the back of the house, but I park half a block down the street. I'd rather not be hemmed in if this gets too boring. I lift a grocery-store cheesecake from the passenger seat and walk past a series of pastel split levels with gingerbread eaves. The sidewalk is cream-white, too new yet to have aged to grey. An older man watering his lawn with a hose watches me cautiously as I go by, and I leave fading hose-water footprints half-way up Ed and Teresa's walk.

There's a heavy door knocker, a thick brass ring in a monkey's mouth. The monkey has exaggerated eyebrows, one of them raised at an unsettling angle. I rap twice, sharply. There's no other way with a brass knocker. I hear muffled shouts and footsteps from inside.

"Jason!" Ed greets me with his usual enthusiasm. "Teresa," he shouts over his shoulder, "your brother's here." He turns back to me. "Come in. You're the first one."

I hold out the cheesecake. "I brought something. Just store-bought." The box wavers at the end of my arm, draped in its white plastic bag. Ed takes it with both hands. "How wonderful," he says with a smile of almost tortured gratitude. "Thanks." You'd think he'd spent his whole day hoping someone would present him with a six-dollar cheesecake. He turns and leads the way to the kitchen.

Teresa is scraping celery-tops from a wooden cutting board into an under-counter bin labelled 'compost.' There is a platter piled high with steaks and a large stainless-steel bowl of potato salad covered with plastic wrap. Maia, their daughter, is bunched in her high chair, fisting Cheerios to her mouth from a plastic Winnie-the-Pooh bowl. Her eyes widen when she sees me.

"Mocha psycho," she says.

"Hey, Jason," Teresa says as she knees the compost bin back out of sight.

"*Mocha* psycho," Maia says again, craning her neck toward her mother, extending a couple of drool-smeared fingers in my approximate direction.

"What's that Maia?" Teresa steps around the counter toward the high chair.

"*Mocha* psycho." Maia's tone is more urgent now, her brow furrowing under her home-cut bangs, her pudgy hand stabbing toward me in awkward bursts. "*Mocha* psycho."

Teresa glances toward me. Then she smiles an exaggerated smile. "That's *right*, honey bunny. *Motor*cycle. Very *goo*-ood." Proud and satisfied, Maia relaxes back into the chair and sticks a finger into a gummy grin.

Teresa turns to me with an apologetic smile. "Guy on the corner got a '66 Triumph from his wife for his fiftieth birthday, rides it up and down the block Saturday afternoons. He has a jacket kind of like yours." She glances around. "Louisa not with you?"

"No, sorry. She's helping run some focus groups for some pharmaceutical company."

While doing research into a treatment for narcolepsy, the drug company had accidentally developed a faster-acting variant of a popular stimulant-based laxative (to the unpleasant surprise of the lab techs who cleaned the chimp cages).[8] They were hoping to position mild constipation as either Adult Onset Rectal Exigency or Recurrent Colorectal Pseudo-obstructive Disorder, depending on which name tested better.

"You're looking well," Ed says to me. "Have you lost weight?" He always says this. If anything I've been gaining. I think he read it in a business-skills book. He also keeps track of peoples' kids' birthdays on his Blackberry.

Bobby, now four, slowly stomps in, his hands raised like claws. "Grrrr," he says to me through a grin. "I'm a big big *ti*-ger." I rear back in mock fear, and he giggles. We do this three or four times, then it's his father's turn, then Teresa's. We are all obligingly afraid of the big big tiger.

"Come see my new patio speakers," Ed says. "Here, we'll put on this Monk re-issue that I just picked up." I follow him into the living room, intrigued. Monk seems a bit adventurous for Ed. Bobby stomps after us. "*Five* little *mon*-keys *jum*-ping on the *bed*," he chants, not quite in rhythm with his steps. "*One* fell *off* and *bumped* his *head*."

Ed slides a CD case from a tall black rack next to his brushed aluminum stereo stand. He waves a hand, and his CD player's motion-sensitive cover glides open.

"*Ma*-ma called the *doc*-tor and the *doc*-tor said."

I scan the rack for the beige edge of my CBC recording, spot it

---

8. Apparently some corner-office silverback with a reputation for both off-the-wall innovative thinking and clawing-the-wall benders confused the two different types of stimulants one foggy Monday morning, and the drones in the lab just assumed he was ahead of the curve.

near the bottom. Still there. Ed gently lays the Monk in place. Bobby makes a stern face and shakes his finger. "*No* more *mon*-keys *jum*-ping on the *bed.*"

Ed touches a glassy button, and a half dozen variously-sized speakers surround us with the intro to '*Round Midnight*. He makes an imperceptible volume correction, then heads back through the kitchen toward the deck and the yard. "Come get a beer and we'll go outside," he says. Bobby stomps behind us. "*Four* little *mon*-keys *jum*-ping on the *bed.*"

"Um, actually ..." I start to say, but he has already disappeared into the kitchen. By the time I catch up to him he's coming out of the fridge with a dark green bottle about the size and shape of an oil filter. "Here, try this new microbrew," he says, holding it out to me. "It's made with Brazil nuts and fennel."

Teresa doesn't even look up from the carrot that she's hollowing out. "Jason doesn't drink, Ed. Remember?"

Ed purses his lips and makes a little *oops* shrug. "Right, sorry." He sticks his head back in the fridge. "Let's see. Coke, Sprite? Mango juice? Cranberry? Organic goat's milk?"

"*One* fell *off* and *bumped* his *head.*"

I take a can of Sprite and pop it open as we carry on toward the sliding door.

"Have a look at the new fence while you're back there," Teresa says. "Cedar."

Ed opens the sliding door. "Weathers better than that pressure-treated stuff."

"*Ma*-ma called the *doc*-tor and the *doc*-tor said."

We step onto the deck. "There," Ed says, pointing to two rubber-rimmed hemispheres high on the exterior wall about ten feet apart.

"*No* more *mon*-keys *jum*-ping on the *bed.*"

For their size the speakers are pretty good: rich piano over-tones, bass only slightly muddy. "Nice sound," I say.

Ed grins. "I had to order them from Germany."

I back down the steps onto the lawn, listening as I go. The sound carries well, though I wonder if the hose guy next door appreciates it.

"*Three* little *mon*-keys *jum*-ping on the *bed*."

"Hey," I say. On the driveway side of the house the new cedar fence arches up over a seven-foot circular hole. "A moon gate."

"Yeah. Good call. Touch of tradition, as far as it goes," Ed says. "Nothing too aggressive, to upset the horsey neighbours. So I had to have a guy come in and drill right through the brick to get the speaker wires out ..."

The sun is low by the time Ed gets the food started, and most of the backyard is in shade. A couple of women put sweaters on. I'm on grill duty, making flipper-jabs under the steaks to keep them from sticking. Ed, who at the moment is hauling more ice out to the beer cooler, will decide when they actually need to be flipped.

A silhouette appears in the moon gate, in the corner of my eye. She hesitates, framed by the sun, one hand resting lightly on the cedar, and scans the shadowy yard. Then she steps out of the glare and takes shape.

"Judy!" Ed says, packing ice around green bottles with his hands. "You made it." He wipes the ice-water on his khakis and walks toward her.

She's tall and slim, with the narrow face and long hands of some thoughtful, languid profession. Cellist. Librarian. Ballet dancer.

"Judy, Jason. Jason, Judy." And then Ed is off to trim the parsley, or whatever.

Judy is Ed's cousin. An assistant professor—very junior, she assures me, as we sit with our paper plates on the steps of Ed's deck —in the Asian Studies department at the University.

She's delightful.

"I hardly ever see Ed and Teresa. Couple times a year maybe. I don't know why. They're great, aren't they?" She stabs a plastic fork into a chunk of potato salad. "How do you know them?"

"I'm Teresa's brother."

She looks at me directly for the first time. "Oh!" she says, brightening with interest, pointing at me with the potato fork. "You're the composer!"

"That's me." Nice to be recognized.

"I have that album," she says, and I feel a warmth in my chest. This delightful woman has my album. "Ed gave it to me. I use it in my classes sometimes. 'Asian influences in modern music' sort of thing."

The warmth in my chest fades a little. Asian influences? My piece doesn't have an Asian bone in its body.

"What?" Judy says.

Uh oh. I've gone too long without responding. Now my non-response has taken on a meaning, and I'm not even sure what that meaning is.

"Um," I say, stalling for time. It doesn't get me much, so I say it again. "Um ..."

Just say what you're thinking. You're never going to see this woman again.

"Um, nothing. Just thinking my piece probably isn't much use to you for that."

"Oh." She realizes what she's said—or how I've *taken* what she's said—and she gets charmingly flustered. "Oh, no, sorry, listen, that's not what I was getting at. Really. I listen to the whole album in the car. I like it your piece. It's good."

"Mmm-*hm*," I say with a little smile. "And what's it called? My piece?"

She pauses, looks at me. "Um," she says.

I wait.

Nothing else. Finally she shrugs her shoulders and laughs. "I don't remember. Sorry."

I raise an expectant eyebrow. "In-*fer*-nal ..." I say in a singsongy *come on now, you can do it* sort of tone.

"Damn you," she says with a laugh. "I *listen* in the car, I don't read liner notes. Infernal. Hmm. Infernal. Nghhhh!" She grunts in frustration. "Infernal *Sonata?*"

"Nope. Try again."

"You're a rotten bastard," she says, smiling. "Infernal Suite?"

"Nope."

"Infernal Concerto?"

"Nope."

"OK, I give up. Infernal Two-step. Infernal Haiku. Infernal Bog-trot. Infernal—"

"Variations."

She slaps her leg. "*Thank* you. Infernal *variations.*" A couple of people look up at us from across the lawn. She lowers her voice. "You're right, though. They're not all that Asian, are they?"

"Not unless Dante was from China."

She smiles again. "Yeah, well." She saws off a narrow wedge of steak with her plastic knife and puts it in her mouth. "I'm hardly one to talk," she says, chewing.

"What do you mean? You're a professor of Asian Studies."

"Mmm-hmm," she says, still chewing. "Came to it late, though." She swallows. "In my teens I was all Tiffany and Michael Jackson and Duran Duran. You couldn't get me near anything Chinese."

Ed catches this last bit as he stops by carrying a platter with more steaks. "Boy, is *that* true. I remember you crying all the way to calligraphy lessons every Saturday morning. You wanted to take swimming lessons instead, like your friend Mona."

Judy chuckles. "Great-great-grandfather would have been appalled."

I must've looked puzzled.

"He was with Zhou Enlai in Paris in the twenties," Ed says. "We heard about it at pretty much every family gathering, growing up." He smiles at Judy, an insider smile.

Judy puts on a deep, mimicking voice. "Your great-great-grandfather helped set up the Calgary branch of the *Cheekungtong* at the turn of the century," she says, and Ed laughs. It makes me sad somehow. I didn't know Zhou Enlai was ever *in* Paris. I don't know what the cheeky-whatsit is.

"I didn't have quite that family connection growing up," I finally say.

Ed nods toward his cousin. "There's the source. Pretty much everything Teresa knows about China she learned from Judy."

Judy raises an affirmative eyebrow. "If it's something you're interested in ...?"

"Well," I say, hesitating. Deciding. Thinking about Aunt Jasmine's moon cakes. About knobbly rocks in a Montreal garden.

She smiles at me with those delightful eyes. "I have a couple of books I can lend you to get you started."

She gives me her card, with her phone number at the University.

"*Infernal Variations* is going to be in a movie," I say.

And somehow the subject of Louisa just never comes up.

We meet three times, at the University library, during the day. It's safe. Innocent. I've told Louisa that Ed's cousin is teaching me about China. She's delighted. I haven't mentioned that Ed's cousin's is a woman. But why would I?

The first meeting is a basic run-through of the dynasties, from antiquity to the beginning of the current century. Or the last century, I guess we'll have to start saying in a couple of months, with Y2K looming. I haven't done anything to prepare for it since that dinner with Miranda and Anton, which still gives me a creepy chill every once in a while.

The second meeting is more cultural. Bronze vessels, Tang poetry. Confucian classics. She touches on music. "I have a pretty good collection of recordings. You might find something you can use in your own music. You could do some settings of Li Po or—Ooh, I know!" She pulls out her diary and her pen.

"What?"

"I'm making a note to lend you *Journey to the West*."

"Is that a piece of music?"

"It's a literary work. Big Chinese epic. Maybe it'll inspire you like Dante did."

"How are the China lessons coming?" Louisa asks one evening over the top of the *Herald*'s entertainment section.

"Fine." I'm at the dining room table, assembling my balsa wood Oratory. It's trickier than I'd expected.

"There's an exhibit of modern Asian art at the Glenbow, if you're interested?"

"Sure. That sounds nice."

My third meeting with Judy feels more charged. She starts with the 1911 Republican Revolution, and by the time of the Japanese invasion and World War II her knee is brushing mine under the table. When Mao proclaims the People's Republic in 1949, she asks me if I'd like to meet her for a drink sometime. She could play me some of her recordings, if I'm interested.

Now is the time to say something, if I'm going to.

All I say is that that sounds nice.

We had a couple of playground toys in our back yard, but Dad let them get pretty wrecked pretty fast. The wooden swing-seat hung limply from a single chain, and the plastic slide was split about halfway down. We didn't care. The swing was our Tarzan rope, and we all just learned to rise up on one bum-cheek as we slid down the slide.

One Sunday afternoon my cousin Danny didn't rise up soon enough. The corner of his patch-pocket snagged the crack and spun him sharply to the left. There was a brief ripping sound, and he rolled barrel-like off the end of the slide, landing on his shoulder in the dirt. "Uhhfff," he said. Little hard candies from his flapping pocket tinkled after him.

Danny's sister Lynne, two years younger, stood there stunned. Teresa was busy hanging by her knees from the poplar tree and didn't even notice. She was already close to six feet by then.

I laughed.

That was a mistake.

Two weekends later I was sitting in the space between our garage and the fence, ploughing ditches in the sand with a tiny bulldozer. I could tell Lynne's walk before I saw her, as she came up our driveway. "D'you want to come and play with Danny and me?"

An ant wandered into my little ditch, and I bulldozed sand on top of it. "I guess." I got up and followed her across the street.

"He's in the shed," she said as we crossed their back yard. It was an old home-built shed, flat brown, plywood over a stud frame. It was big enough for a car if you could get one there across the patchy grass. The door was white, with two wooden Xs and a hook-and-eye closure. We went in and Lynne slammed it behind us. The only light was from the dusty screened window at the back, over the workbench.

"Who said *you* could come here mister China *man?*" Danny was sitting on the bench, his head a shadow.

"He was burying ants in the sand." Lynne giggled.

Two or three other neighbourhood kids were also sitting in the shadows, on upended buckets or stacks of snow tires, staring

"Say something in Chinese mister chinky China *man*," Danny said.

"Hung dung fung dung," one of the other kids said, pulling his eyes at the corners and laughing.

"No," Lynne said, starting to get uncomfortable. "His eyes aren't *like* that."

Danny laughed. "You're right. His eyes are the only part of him that's *normal*."

All of the kids laughed at that. Except maybe Lynne.

"I'm not a China man, I'm French! My Daddy's French, so I'm French!"

Danny stared. Then he laughed, looking around at the others. "His *Daaad*dy. His *Daaad*dy's French so he's French. All right then mister French *man*, say something in *French* then."

But of course I couldn't.

Danny actually turned out all right. He and his wife Sue have a vegetarian restaurant on Fourth Street. They give to Amnesty and canvass for Heart and Stroke, and their son goes to the Waldorf school.

It's just another meeting with Ed's cousin. Who's teaching me about China. It's nothing unusual.

"Have fun," Louisa says cheerfully as I open the door to go out.

"Thanks," I say, kind of flatly. "I might stop somewhere for a coffee after."

It's nothing unusual.

"If I'm asleep when you get home, try to be quiet."

"Okay. Fine. See you."

I close the door behind me.

Judy is on a stool at the bar with her legs crossed, drawing a fingertip across the condensation on her wine glass. It leaves a horizontal amber line, backlit against the surrounding mist. She's wearing charcoal stockings and a slit skirt open to her hip. She turns her head, sees me and smiles.

"Exotic is a bad stereotype," I say as I take the next stool.

"It's cotton, not silk," she says, turning back to her glass. "Besides, I'm not even wearing lipstick." She's right, she isn't. She doesn't need to. She draws a second line, from the rim down, through the middle of the first one. An amber cross.

As I take the stool beside her my leg touches her knee, and she presses it against me. There's a flutter in my genitals. I stare at her glass. Cross. Crossroads.

Just a meeting with Ed's cousin. Nothing unusual.

Judy's apartment is on the umpteenth floor of a tower across the tracks from downtown. The breeze on the balcony stirs the dark edges of her hair. I look away—down, toward the street—and lurch back, stomach tight, sweat beading on my forehead.

"Are you all right?" She touches my elbow to steady me, and it tingles.

"Heights." The moisture on my face and neck dries cold.

"Let's go in then. It's a bit chilly anyhow." Her hand rests on my shoulder, guiding me through the sliding doors. "I get that myself, sometimes. Panicky feeling, like you're going to fall." She closes the balcony door, sealing us in.

She offers me more tea. Chinese tea. She's drinking the same California chardonnay she'd ordered at the bar.

"Thanks, just a bit."

She disappears into the kitchen as I perch on her couch. When she comes back she has kicked off her shoes. She gently refills my cup and sets the teapot on the floor by the stereo. "Why don't we start with the *dizu*?" she says. "A wooden flute." She inserts a CD, presses a button, fiddles with the volume. "The *dizu* has a small vibrating membrane, a little like the kazoo, but it doesn't sound at all kazoo-like." She crosses to the couch and sits next to me.

Simple flute-sounds ease from the speakers. My hands are damp, my pulse racketing in my head.

"You're right," I say, after a while. "There's a richness to it, but not a harsh edge." She draws her feet onto the couch and leans her head against my arm.

It isn't a fear of falling. The unease I felt on the balcony. It's a fear of jumping.

In the pause between two tracks her hand rests on my thigh. I turn toward rising lips and a breath of chardonnay.

What the fuck am I doing?

"Listen," Judy says afterward, earnestly, with her face against my neck and her hair across my chest. "I'm, ah. See, I just got out of." She shakes her head a little. Her hair feels nice as it shifts against my skin. "This was nice, don't get me wrong. I'm just." Another nice little hair shift. "I'm just not really looking to start anything too, um, you know." She looks up. "I hope that's okay."

A small sigh of relief escapes my chest. Not audible I hope. "Hmm. Yeah," I say. "I guess that's okay."

And of course it is. It's brilliant. It's the solution.

It's the solution before I even acknowledge the problem.

The partial solution.

Louisa is asleep when I get home. I give myself a quiet sponge bath in the washroom before I go to bed, and rinse out the facecloth thoroughly before I drape it over the back of my laundry hamper.

And in the morning we're both rushing to get moving, and what time I got home last night doesn't even come up.

Six

Heilongjiang Province

The man spots another rock in the scrubby field, one the size of his own head, half sunk in the muck. He claws the earth away from the sides until it's exposed enough that he can lever it out with a stick. He lifts it to his midsection, then presses it up onto his shoulder and balances it there. It must be five hundred metres to the roadside, where the cadre said the rocks were to be collected. He takes one step, then another. When he reaches the pile he tips the rock from his shoulder and steps back. It clacks against the others, rolls a bit, settles.

That should be it. He has criss-crossed the whole field. There are no more.

The cadre pulls up in an official vehicle. "Why are these rocks here?" he asks without preamble.

"This is where you said to put them."

"Nonsense. They are too close to the road." The cadre is lying. He said to put them here. "They should be over there, near that hut." He points north, to a spot a hundred metres away. "See to it," he says as the vehicle pulls away.

The man looks at the hut. He looks at the rocks. The pile is as high as his knees, and as wide as the road.

Uncle Larry left Canada when I was five. I don't really remember his actual leaving, which I think was kept from me, but I remember the tensions it was hidden behind. Or I think I do. Maybe I just remember hearing things later, quietly. Indirectly.

But I'm pretty sure I remember Mama crying behind a closed door, and Dad shouting, and a slapping sound followed by a frightening silence. I'm pretty sure I remember asking Teresa what *chink boyfriend* meant, and Teresa fiercely telling me to shut up.

Judy and I are having lunch at a vegetarian dim sum restaurant on the edge of Chinatown and I'm thinking about the tattoo in the small of her back. The wall-mounted speakers are playing 'Candle in the Wind' on pan-pipes. She's educating me about the Great Leap Forward, Mao's grand plan at the end of the fifties to jump-start economic growth through mass agricultural development and backyard iron mills.

"So what are those characters tattooed on your back, anyhow?"

"Jesus, Lavoie, keep your focus. Twenty million people starved to death. It's something you should know about." Our table is covered with little bamboo baskets of mock chicken and sticky rice, and fat dumplings stuffed with baby bok choy.

"I am keeping my focus. Keeping it on imagining you naked. And then I wonder about the tattoo."

She raps my forehead with the back end of a chopstick. "Fine. If I tell you, can we get back to Mao?"

I make a mock-contemplative frown. "We'll see."

She snorts. "It's the mantra from the Heart Sutra, in Chinese."

I must look baffled.

"You know, the Heart Sutra? Form is emptiness, emptiness is form?"

Nothing.

She looks at me the way you might look at a fourteen-year-old who's never heard of Miles Davis or Sir Wilfrid Laurier.

"Here," she says, rooting in her purse, "I have the romanized version lasered on my key ring." There's a jangle as she fishes it out and passes it across the table to me, the fob of the ring an oblong of dark-stained wood with four short lines of precisely incised script.

"Buddhist?" I ask, and she nods.

"Gate, gate—" I start to read, but she laughs and cuts me off. "Not 'gate' like a gate in a fence. *Gah*-teh."

"*Gate gate*," I read. *Gah*-teh *gah*-teh.

"Right. Gone, gone."

"*Paragate?*"

"Gone beyond."

"*Parasamgate?*"

A small chuckle. "Close enough. Gone entirely beyond."

"*Bodhi, svaha?*"

An approving nod. "*Bodhi* meaning to awaken, and *svaha* a kind of exclamation of wonder."

"Like 'hot damn'?"

She looks down and shakes her head, smiling. "Sure fine. Something like that."

"Gone beyond what?"

She shrugs. "Everything, I guess."

I pick a dumpling from a basket and swirl it in a dish of something yellow. Some kind of mustard. "You guess? What kind of Buddhist are you, then?"

"I'm not, really." She lifts a thumb-sized clump of rice to her mouth and pops it in. "More a cultural thing," she says as she chews, swallows. "The Heart Sutra is important in the Chan sect. Which the Japanese took Zen from," she adds, smiling mischievously, "and mass-marketed the hell out of."

"Zen I've heard of," I say. I hold up the key fob. "But this isn't Chinese?"

She shakes her head. "Sanskrit."

"Any chance I can see the Chinese version again when we're done here?"

She raises an eyebrow and stares at me, amused despite herself. "OK listen," she finally says as she lifts a glistening white rice-flour tube from a side plate with her chopsticks, "I have a monograph that provides a decent overview of the Great Leap. If you're not up for a history lesson tonight then I can get it to you later. You know what?" She dips the tube in soy sauce and lifts it to her mouth. "I still don't have your number." She takes a bite.

I square my folded napkin against the edge of the table, beside my plate. I arrange my chopsticks on it, parallel to its long side. "Let me give you my cell number."

She carefully places the rest of the white tube onto her plate. "You don't want to give me your home number? What, are you married or something?"

It's a joke, but the pause is just long enough. Just too long.

A server passes with someone else's tea. Judy's face closes like a claw.

"Do you have something to tell me?"

My mouth opens, but the words cramp in my throat.

"You creeping little bastard," she says. "God!" She shakes her head and flops back against the booth. "Guys," she says to the ceiling. "Fuck."

"Listen," I say. "I mean, it's just. It sort of."

I stop.

"Yeah. That's probably just about it, isn't it?"

We're quiet for a while, taking in what just happened, this revelation.

For her, the content of it.

For me, the fact of it.

"No wonder you sounded so relieved the other night." Her eyes are focused on the wall.

There's a long silence. Neither of us eats anything else. It would be disrespectful somehow. Dishes clatter in the kitchen. A car with tinted windows goes by outside. A man at the next table takes off his glasses and cleans his ear with one end. The pointless shit you notice in important moments.

Judy's lips tighten.

"God *damn* it, Jason. I really *liked* you."

And the kick that she gives my shin on the word *liked* really hurts.

And she never does lend me that *Journey to the West* thing.

I don't know if Mama's decline began with Uncle Larry's leaving or if that's just a tempting way to account for it in hindsight, but there's something that feels right about the idea. Before he left I don't remember so much shouting, for example, or Mama sleeping during the day in the recliner, or on the couch, or on the laundry room floor. Or the strangely heavy cereal boxes that turned out to have brown screw-topped bottles nestled against their wax paper bags of Froot Loops or Frankenberry.

But then how much can any of us remember from before we were five?

Ephraim Grant's action film premieres in the fall, to get the jump on the Christmas blockbuster season. The deal my Toronto entertainment lawyer got me didn't extend to the red carpet in L.A., but it did run to a block of V.I.P. passes to the first Calgary screening. The theatre has blocked off two rows about half-way back, with crisp cardboard 'Reserved' signs at each end. We even get complementary concession food served to us at our seats.

We don't fill both rows, but we make a decent effort: myself and Louisa, Sleeve and his current girlfriend Pammy (a faun-eyed bank teller who gets all of her calcium from non-fat lattes and all of her news from *Entertainment Tonight*), Miranda and her husband, plus three people from work and their respective spouses/dates, plus a handful of local musicians whom I sometimes work with, including Bill the cellist from the original CBC recording, who has driven down from St. Albert for the occasion.

The plot is skeletal. A rogue ex-Soviet colonel has commandeered a missile silo somewhere in Central Asia. The hero, a disgraced FBI profiler who has wrongly taken the fall over the recent assassination of the Secretary of Defense, figures out that the silo is a decoy for the setting off of a suitcase nuke at the Lincoln Memorial, but no-one believes him except the Colonel's beautiful Kazakh niece, an internationally renowned concert flautist. Then stuff starts to blow up.

Bill and I catch it first: the cello tremolo from the beginning of the 'river of boiling blood' section. We start a chain of nudging and whispering down our row as the camera cuts back and forth between the hero's stolen Hummer and the Colonel's musclebound henchman at the wheel of a panel van packed with salvaged pre-war dynamite. Eventually the henchman's evasive weaving exposes his left front tire to a clear shot from the hero's trademark vintage Smith and Wesson, and a series of sharp violin attacks steers the out-of-control van over a growling cello and viola fugato and into a bridge abutment, where it gloriously explodes.

And I start to cry.

Weeks go by—brewing and serving coffee, settling back into normalcy with Louisa after the increasingly-remote-seeming Judy tangent, finishing the intricate balsa wood Oratory and displaying it on top of the dining room bookcase—and I still can't seem to get anywhere with the opera.

I have this idea for a plaintive solo violin at the beginning of one of the scenes, something Chinese-sounding, but after four hours of writing and rewriting it still sounds like Debussy. I just don't know enough about what I'm trying to do. I need to stop writing and do some listening.

I drive to a small mall in Chinatown where I remember Judy pointing out a store with recordings of traditional music. I park near the Calgary Chinese Cultural Centre. Judy once told me it's a replica of one of the buildings at the Temple of Heaven in Beijing. She said they brought craftsmen from China to build it using traditional construction methods. I keep meaning to look into the courses they offer in Chinese culture—again, something Judy told me about —but somehow I never do.

I cross the street and wander through the mall, trying to remember where the CD store is. There's a food store, with yams and Chinese broccoli and gnarled, dried things that I can't identify. There's a travel agency with its signs mostly in Chinese. There's a store with painted fans and silk scrolls and carvings of Buddhas and dragons.

And standing at the counter, holding her hand out for her change, is Judy.

I stop, back up a step. I'll slip away before she sees me. But then she glances up. She looks startled for a moment, looks away, then seems to realize that she can't pretend not to have seen me. She raises a hand in a tentative wave. I wave back.

She thanks the clerk in Cantonese and comes out toward me. "Papercuts for my niece in Toronto," she says, holding up a small, flat paper bag. "Panda bears."

I nod. "How old's your niece?"

"Six."

"Mmmm."

We stand there, not speaking, not meeting each other's eyes. She's wearing a gold silk blouse with embroidered animal figures on either side of the scoop neckline. Monkeys, judging by the tails that trace the outside curve of each breast.

"So, asshole," she finally says—not bitterly; just in an ordinary tone like it's somehow my actual nickname. "What brings you down here?"

"Um, CDs. Inspiration. I want something with that Chinese instrument that sounds kind of like a violin."

"The *erhu*."

"Yeah. But I can't remember where that store is you showed me."

She scowls and shakes her head—the long-suffering teacher faced yet again with the idiot pupil. "Follow me. I'm heading that way anyhow."

I can't be sure when Mama's decline began, but I'm clear on when it ended. It ended under a gold-tiled Chinese gate in the fading daylight.

Judy takes me to the CD store and, sceptical about my judgment, comes in to help me pick something out. I end up buying three, two with *erhu* music and one with various Chinese flutes, which is more than I can comfortably afford, but it's strangely nice doing something companionable together again.

The teenaged cashier says something to me in Cantonese as she puts the discs into a small blue bag, and Judy responds to it quickly and smoothly, easing us all through the moment before it has a chance to get awkward. The two of them have a short, amicable conversation in Cantonese, each glancing in my direction. The cashier hands me the bag with both hands and a small bow, and thanks me in English. They have a final brief exchange in Cantonese and wave to each other as we leave the store.

"What was that all about?"

Judy chuckles. It sounds nice. "She thinks you're cute. Something about your eyes."

I look back toward the store. "Cool. So why didn't she tell me that in English?"

"It was meant as a compliment to me, actually. She thought we were together."

We go into a small tea shop and make harmless conversation over cups of oolong. Our knees brush under the tiny table. Judy doesn't seem to have been heading anywhere after all. Eventually she looks at me and shakes her head. "You are such a shit, you know."

"I know it."

When our tea is done she asks how I got there. I confess to having my car. She confesses to needing a ride home. We leave the mall together. I hold the door for her, and her shoulder brushes my bare forearm as she passes. She smiles and looks away. "So where are you parked?"

I gesture with my CD bag. "Over there, by the building with the blue roof."

"The Chinese Cultural Centre," she says as we cross the street. "They have courses. You should check it out."

"Thanks," I say, not bothering to remind her that she's told me this before.

"That peaked dome, with the dark blue roof tiles? It's a replica of the Hall of Prayers at the Temple of Heaven, in Beijing. They built it according to traditional Chinese architectural principles, using expert craftsmen from China."

I don't bother reminding her that she's told me that before either. My eyes are following the curve of the leftmost monkey's tail around her leftmost breast.

We get to my car. I unlock the doors. We get in. I drive to her apartment.

Knowing it's stupid, she asks me up. Knowing it's stupid, I agree. And soon, to the sound of the *erhu*, we're stupidly having sex on her living room carpet.

Immediately afterward we realize what a mistake it is.

"How did that happen?" she says.

"I don't know. It just happened."

Then it just happens again.

"Your uncle just disappeared?"

The sun is going down, shadows lengthening through Judy's bedroom window. I'll have to head home soon. "As far as we know. He went to China when I was five and after a while no-one heard from him again."

"What year was that?"

"Around 1975."

"Why did he go?"

I shrug, jostling her head against my chest. "I don't know. Something about Deng Xiaoping, I think. If I'm remembering right. If I heard it right in the first place."

"Hmmm. Was he idealistic?"

"I was five. How would I know?" Then I think about the hot pool in Banff, the Japanese store signs. The burger and the milkshake. "Yeah, he probably was. Why?"

She runs a finger around my nipple. "Just a thought. Deng was on the rise in 1975. Reforms seemed likely. It was a promising time for idealists, even in the diaspora. Especially in the diaspora." She stops her finger, then runs it in the opposite direction, looks up at me. "Maybe he wanted to be a part of it."

And so we're back pretty much where we were all those weeks ago, like nothing happened. Except now Judy knows. There's a new edge to how she talks to me, now that she knows. Not contempt, exactly. It's more genial than that. A sort of pretend rudeness that isn't quite pretend, that she seems to feel entitled to now, like I have no right to complain. Which I guess I don't.

"Just stay put," she says one day after one of our 'lessons.' "I want to change my answering machine." She presses a button —*beep*—on the bedside machine and speaks into a plastic grille, recording a hokey Christmas message about leaving your tidings of comfort and joy after the tone. Even that somehow makes me hot. What the hell's the matter with me?

Judy gets that we won't see each other at Christmas, so she gives me my gift early. It's wrapped in bright red paper with darker red ideograms on it. I can tell by the feel that it's a book.

"Open it."

It's a copy of the *I Ching*. It has a grey dust jacket over a bright yellow cover.

"You don't have it already, do you?"

"Um, no. I'm not even sure what it is." I flip through it. Symbols made of horizontal lines. Paragraphs of text broken up by little verses of poetry or something.

"It's one of the classics. Part wisdom book, part oracle. You can use it for divination if you want to." She says this last bit with a nervous chuckle, like she's half serious, but half worried I'll think she's peddling some new age hooey. Plausible deniability. "The instructions are in there. There's a complicated way using yarrow stalks, but most people just use coins."

She presses three antique Chinese coins into my hand. Round, with square holes in the middle.

They're beautiful. And they make me sad.

A couple of weeks before New Year's I'm finally doing something about Y2K, and Louisa is grudgingly indulging me. We've been to Zellers for extra blankets and to Canadian Tire for collapsible water containers and a chemical toilet about the size of a snare drum. Now we're at Safeway.

"*Two* flats of baked beans?" she says with a raised eyebrow as I lift them down from the bulk shelf. Her feigned exasperation gets a little less feigned each time.

I manoeuvre the flats into the buggy. "You might not be so cavalier about protein once the world economy stalls and the stores empty out." The anxiety has totally overtaken me. "One meal for the two of us per can, that's more than three weeks right there, lunch and dinner. What about beef jerky?" I peer between the pillow-sized bags of rice and the gallon cans of tomato sauce. "Do they have bulk beef jerky?"

Louisa thinks I'm overreacting. Like Miranda with Anton, though Louisa probably wouldn't appreciate the comparison. "We're not going to need all this stuff, Jason," she says for about the eleventh time. "The computers aren't going to turn into pumpkins at midnight New Year's Eve."

"I'm not saying they will. I'm just saying we need to be ready in *case* they do." I reach into a cardboard crate in the middle of the aisle and lift out two ten-litre bottles of spring water by their plastic handles.

"So then why not get a crossbow in case the meat runs out, or a pair of size 17 quintuple-E shoes in case your feet get flattened by, I don't know ..." She shakes her head and chuckles. " ... stampeding *zombies* or something?"

I drop the bottles loudly onto the flats of beans. "I'm just being prudent. The world economy is based on electronic communication. If it goes down we could be fucked if we're not prepared."

"The world economy is based on breasts and snacks." She gestures toward the magazine racks and the rows of chips near the checkouts. "Neither one needs a computer."

"Shipping them does," I say with a grunt, heaving two flats of canned corn to the edge a shelf. The top one shifts, and I take an awkward step back. "How do you think those things got here? Invoices, manifests. Things with numbers and destinations and dates." I jostle the flats to move the top one back, but it won't budge. "If the —*gnhhh*, Jesus!"—another jostle, another step backward—"if the computers all go mental, where does that leave all the canned corn and the breast magazines and the jalapeno sour cream tortilla chips?"

"They're fixing that."

"How do we know?" I hold the bottom flat with one knee while I try tilting them to line them up. "How do we know it'll be enough?"

And as I finally balance the flats and turn them toward the cart I notice someone peering in at our purchases.

"I don't see any ammunition," Judy says.

Thankfully, my sweating and shortness of breath are consistent with wrestling the corn into the cart. I take a moment to recover and then make reasonably smooth introductions. As smooth as they can be with this heart rate. Fuck. Fuck fuck fuck.

"Isn't that funny?" Louisa says after she and Judy have shaken hands. "I don't know why, but I just assumed that Ed's cousin was a man."

"Wasn't I clear about that?" I think my voice is reasonably even.

"One of those assumptions that we make about professionals, I guess," Judy says, maybe a bit too brightly. Or maybe my radar for that sort of thing is just *way* off the dial right now.

"Right," Louisa says, "like that story about the boy who's in the accident—"

"—and the doctor's his mother," Judy says. "Yeah. Like that."

I pull at the grocery list in Louisa's hand. "OK, so anyhow, we still need the freeze-dried chili, the bulk candles—"

"No, stop right there," Louisa says. "I'm not playing any more."

A jolt of panic rattles my chest. What has she noticed?

"You want to play end of the world," she says, handing me the list, "knock yourself out. But I'm done for today."

I almost cry. She's talking about groceries.

She turns to Judy. Finally. A quick "goodbye, nice to have met you" and I'll be able to unclench my ass.

"You want to get a coffee?" Louisa asks.

My hairline prickles with sweat. "We can't," I say. "Um. The ice." I point to the list. Eight bags of ice. "It'll melt in the car."

Louisa looks at me sideways. "All right then, survival boy, how's this? You go home and look after your ice and your beans, and your fifteen cartons of strawberry granola bars, and I find my own way home. After Judy and I have coffee."

I flash Judy a tiny pleading glance.

"I can give her a ride," she says with an amused little smile.

On my way to the exit I pass what appears to be a locked utility room. "Door is Alarmed" says an eye-level sign. Underneath, in blue marker, someone has written "Window is kind of jittery too."

Yeah. Lot of that going around.

I don't know how I get home or put away the groceries. I obviously must have driven, taken the elevator, carried the flats and the bags and the bottles. No memory of it at all. I am all but comatose as I wait, like I've shorted out. I half expect myself to smell of ozone and acrid smoke. It is all I can do to sit in the armchair instead of curl in a ball in the corner.

Louisa arrives home about an hour after I do. It feels like longer. My radar is cranked past human endurance, but everything seems perfectly normal. She observes in a non-committal way that Judy seems nice, and I equally non-committally agree, and that pretty much seems to be that.

Except that the next morning Judy's business card—the one I've been careful not to have, the one with both her office and home numbers—is somehow on the front of our refrigerator, behind Louisa's Scorpio fridge magnet.

I have a mad urge to ask Louisa to marry me, or buy a house together, or make a baby, but I recognize it as a panic reaction and push it down.

This was too close.

This can't happen.

This has to stop.

"Don't worry," Judy says when I go to see her the next evening, as soon as she opens the door to her apartment. "I didn't blow your cover."

"Thanks," I say. It seems slightly inappropriate. Plus she must already know that I know that.

"Your girlfriend seems sweet, and smart," she says as she closes and chains the door. "Remind me why you're fucking around on her again?"

I'm not clear on that myself.

"I'm not clear on that myself," I say.

I pause. She turns to face me.

"Do you want to stop?" I say. I mean to say *we should stop*, but it doesn't come out that way.

She stares into my eyes for a long time, invasively, like she's hunting for something. Then she grabs my face with both hands and kisses me, hard, wrapping a leg around my waist and drawing me toward her. The kiss goes on for a while, so hard that my lips hurt against my teeth. So hard I worry that they might actually bleed.

Then it stops. She draws back a little, so slightly that our faces are still almost touching. I can feel her breath on my lips.

"I think I want to," she says. "But I don't think I'm going to."

I couldn't have said it better.

Fuck.

I finally tell Sleeve what's going on, over a coffee one evening before Christmas. Some other coffee place, not where I work.

He's kind of surprised, which I guess is understandable.

"What about Louisa?" he asks right away.

"Don't," I say sharply.

"But what if she finds out?"

"*Don't.*" The edge in my tone surprises me a little. It apparently surprises Sleeve, too. He looks at me like I just spit on him. Which I suppose I might have. Hard consonant. I ease up. "Seriously, I just don't let myself think about it. I can't." Even now it has my back damp with sweat, my head heavy and thick. "Why does it have to be about her?" I add lamely.

Sleeve looks at me in a worried kind of way. "Dude, you're living together."

This from *Sleeve.* Jesus.

I don't say anything. I just get up and leave.

I sit up in the armchair all night. Can't sleep. Can't think.

Louisa probably assumes I'm working on the opera.

Small mercies.

Judy and I are actually still doing the lessons. They seem more important to me than ever, and she still seems pleased to share what she knows. That afternoon it's the Cultural Revolution. We stretch out on her bed with a couple of textbooks. In hindsight, probably not the best spot for instruction, but since the books were on her night table it made a kind of sense at the time.

"So," she says, lying on her side, her shirt riding up to expose a delicious inch of abdomen, "by the mid-sixties Mao was afraid the revolution was slipping into the hands of a political bureaucracy ..."

I keep up as best I can, but by the time she gets to Red Guards' attack on the Four Olds—old ideas, old culture, old customs and old something else that I miss entirely because I'm trying to angle my stare down the front of her shirt—my mind is wandering. By the time we get to Decentralization and the Third Front so are my hands. Judy's half-mock slaps become grabs, and then gropes, and pretty soon hips lift, trousers slide free, and legs push textbooks over the edge of the bed.

"Okay," I murmur into her breast a little later as our heart rates begin to settle, "so Mao tries to purge the Party of capitalist roaders, and the Red Guards spin out of his control. What's the Third Front again?"

Judy lifts her face from the damp pillow and pushes her hair out of her eyes. "He's worried. America's in Vietnam, practically on China's doorstep, and his split with Moscow has him paranoid about the Soviets too. So he decides he needs to do some defensive planning."

"Such as?"

She rolls off of me with a little grunt. "Moving manufacturing into the hinterland. He shifts industrial production from urban centres to hundreds of remote locations in the western provinces.

Which means new rail lines, new mines, new dams. It's an economic disaster."

I dab at myself with a tissue. "Then why does he do it?"

"I told you, he's worried." Apparently I look blank. Again. "Okay, here, look. Let me put in terms that'll hold your attention. This" — she draws the edge of a fingernail up the inside of my right thigh — "is Vietnam. Crawling with capitalist American troops. And this" —she draws another nail across my neck, from my left ear down to my right collarbone— "is the Soviet border, crawling with the betrayers of the revolution."

"Mmm hmmmm," I say.

She leans down to my chest. "So if you're Mao, do you want all of your industrial capacity here?" Her tongue traces a circle around my left nipple. "Or here?" Right nipple.

"Mmmm. Probably not."

She nibbles her way down my abdomen to below my stomach. "How about here?" she murmurs into the damp tangle at the fold of my thigh.

I don't answer. I assume it's rhetorical.

And since after that she can only mumble, that's about as far as we get with our lesson.

When people think of Calgary they think of oil and cattle, but it's also a regional shipping hub. That's why Dad almost always had work, even in the lean, "asshole Trudeau" years of the National Energy Program. There were always goods of some sort moving across loading docks—auto parts, lumber, home furnishings, office supplies—and always a need for someone to get everything to the right part of the warehouse and to keep the paperwork in some kind of order. That was Dad. I guess he was pretty good at it, since he was pretty much always working, though he rarely seemed to keep any particular job for more than a year or two.

By 1986, though, he had been working at the same job for

almost four years, so there was enough money for us to drive to Vancouver that summer and spend two days at Expo 86. I'd just finished Grade 11 and was writing embarrassing poetry with phrases like "every fibre of my being" and "I softly weep."

We had a set of highway bingo cards in the back seat (barn, stop sign, police car and so on, with slide-over red windows) and a picnic hamper in the trunk with some fruit and cheese and three bottles of rye. Before we even reached the Rockies Teresa and I had fought, whined to Dad, been yelled at, and lapsed into sullen silence. I carried on reading a dog-eared James Bond from the library and feeling vaguely carsick, while Teresa did crosswords.

We got to Penticton around the middle of the afternoon and checked into a motel Dad had heard about from some shipper at work: three banks of pink stucco units framing a parking lot and a small pool. Teresa and I sat on webbed lawn chairs at a patio table near the pool's gate while Dad got the plastic-fobbed room keys from the office and Mama pulled the car around to our unit and shakily unlocked the trunk. The pop machine had something called Mister Pibb, which I'd never heard of.

I wasn't sure Mama should be driving, even in the parking lot, considering the level in the bottle I'd watched her lift from the hamper and tip into the paper coffee cup she'd held all the way through the Rogers Pass, but by that stage of things Dad had stopped paying attention and none of us ever said anything anyhow. It may not even have been the first bottle.

We had dinner at a spaghetti restaurant and sat by the pool in the evening light listening to kids splashing, and pretty much nobody spoke. The coffee cup had been replaced by a thick motel tumbler, filled to the rim. Mama was still shaking, off and on. When I'd checked the hamper for cheese before dinner there'd been two more bottles. I had no idea where they'd come from.

It took us a while to get on the road the next morning. Mama slept pretty late. When we finally woke her up it took a while before she was responsive, and even then she zoned in and out. Her shakes seemed to have become more like twitches. "Just leave her be and get these bags in the damn trunk," Dad said. "I gotta do all the friggin' work around here?"

It was late in the day when we got to Vancouver. Mama had vomited twice on the roadside, once on the highway from Princeton to Hope and once at the edge of a farmer's field just before we hit Chilliwack. We stayed in an apartment someone had temporarily walled off into four individual units furnished with camping cots. It smelled like drywall and fresh paint. Pretty soon it also smelled like rye.

I don't remember a lot about Expo itself. I remember that it was colourful, and that it was along the edge of a body of water called False Creek. I remember a geodesic dome with a theatre inside. I remember a gigantic hockey stick and puck. I remember a snack bar with a bush plane sculpted in blue neon lights, where Mama waited for us on the first morning until she got kicked out for doctoring her Coke from the mickey in her purse. After that she mainly waited for us in one of the bars.

We made an early start that first morning, partly because Dad didn't want to us to waste the money he was spending by sitting idle and partly because he didn't want us listening to the young couple having morning sex on the other side of the makeshift drywall.

Dad wasn't normally much of a planner, but at Expo suddenly he was. He spread the map on the floor beside the cots and laid out our day like the siege of Stalingrad. The first morning we'd start at the west end with the Yellow Zone and the Green Zone. We'd go to the U.S.A. and General Motors pavilions and the Great Hall of Ramses II. We'd watch the RCMP Musical Ride. Then we'd go to the pavilions of Britain and Alberta. I'm making most of this up now, of course. As I said, I don't remember much. But I still have the map, and I know my father's tastes.

Then we'd try to find someplace cheap for lunch. Splitting up wasn't an option—it was too crowded and dangerous.

In the afternoon it would be the Pink Zone and the Blue Zone, probably stuff like the U.S.S.R. and Saudi pavilions and whatever was on at the Expo Theatre, if we could get in. Day two would be mostly the Red Zone—Saskatchewan, Australia, Ontario, maybe the Canada Pavilion via SkyTrain—plus whatever we felt like going back to in the zones from day one.

He never mentioned the Purple Zone at the east end, which was dominated by the pavilion of the People's Republic of China, and Teresa smacked my arm when I started to ask.

Of course the "no splitting up" rule only lasted until Mama decided she had to sit down and wait for us at the snack bar, and sorting things out after she got kicked out shook up the rest of the schedule for the day. We still managed to stay more-or-less on target until late on Day 2, though, when things went wildly to hell.

They're right about the excitement of the illicit.

Judy and are on our way back from dinner at the Keg. We had fatty appetizers and big slabs of beef. Half the time her stocking foot was in my crotch under the table.

She keeps trying to undo my zipper all the way back to her place, laughing at my attempts to brush her away, to look nonchalant to the other drivers. I have to hold my jacket over my lap as we cross the foyer and wait for the elevator. An old boy with a laundry basket scowls at us all the way to his floor. By the time Judy unlocks the apartment door we're practically fucking in the hallway. "Get in here," she says, grabbing my belt buckle and dragging me toward the bedroom.

We flop onto the bed together, her nipples pressing through her sweater. She clamps her mouth on mine, gnawing. My hand is up under her bra, hers down behind my belt, fingers like tentacles. Squirming, moist fragments of words.

We twist apart. She pulls her sweater over her head and tosses it to the floor. Before it lands her bra is undone. She arches forward and it drops away. I wriggle out of my t-shirt and we're together again, the softness of her breasts against my chest, my hand down the tight back of her jeans. She undoes them, and with a quick hip-lift and hand movement she's naked.

I stand next to the bed and slide off pants and socks in a single motion. I shake the pants flat and fold them neatly on one corner of the foot of the bed.

"What're you, Martha Stewart?" She grabs the pants and flings them through the bedroom door, into the bathroom across the hall, scattering the contents of my pockets. Change jingles against tile. Something clatters into the sink. "Oops," she says, laughing. What must be my wallet bounces off the doorframe and lands with a crash on her bedside phone. The answering machine beeps. She laughs again and flops onto her back.

"Jesus, Judy. Louisa bought me those pants. For all I know they're in the toilet now."

"You want to rescue your pants, Lavoie, or you want to fuck?"

"Well." I climb on top of her. "If I have to choose ..." There's further squirming as we dispose of my underwear, followed by a pause to put the condom on. I'm barely inside of her when the answering machine beeps again.

"That you?" I ask.

"Yeah, it's my vaginal sonar. You're not deep enough."

"Sorry," I say. "How's *this*?"

"*MMMmpf*! Yeah, that'll do."

We left Mama in the Bavarian Garden in the Green Zone while we took the SkyTrain to the Canada Pavilion. When we came back she was gone. We checked every bar in every zone, and then every un-licensed snack bar. We were about to get started on the washrooms when something occurred to me.

"Hey," Dad yelled as I took off east toward the Purple Zone. "Where the hell're you goin'? We're supposed to stick together."

I got there just after the paramedics arrived.

Half an hour or so later I'm coming back from Judy's bathroom. The pants weren't in the toilet after all. Judy is still sprawled across the wrinkled sheets. I crawl between her legs to where they meet, and I nuzzle. She makes a yummy noise. The phone rings.

"I think I'll let the machine get it," she says.

"I thought you might," I say, indistinctly.

The machine clicks, and her outgoing message begins.

"Jesus, Judy, Louisa bought me those pants. For all I know they're in the toilet now ... You want to rescue your pants, Lavoie, or you want to fuck? ... Well. If I have to choose ..."

"Christ almighty!" She flips over and grabs the phone. "Hello? Hello? ... Hello!!" She turns back toward me. "A click and a dial tone."

I crawl up beside her. "Whose number?"

She pushes a button and peers at the little screen, puzzled. "Yours."

And the world crashes into the sink.

She has to be wrong. It has to be someone else. Anyone else. Her mother, her boss, anyone. "Let me see," I say, forcing calm. I check the number, the time of the call. I check my watch. I check the number again. I'm in the bathroom in two steps.

I hop back out on one foot, pulling up a pant leg.

"Oh Jesus," Judy says. Her face is limp and sorry in the light from the hall.

My head hurts. I can hardly see to drive.

Expo's China Gate was a massive arched structure with gold roof tiles and three levels of painted woodwork. It was later donated to Vancouver by the Chinese Government. It's now on Pender Street in Chinatown, where it has deteriorated to the point where I think they're talking about tearing it down.

When I got there a wiry black man in a paramedic uniform was gently prying Mama's arms from one of its round red pillars. Through the middle arch I could see the lights on the grid lines of the geodesic dome blink on against the indigo sky. Mama's eyes were open but unfocused, and one of her legs was trembling. The near side of her face sagged like melting snow.

"Mama!" The paramedic let me by almost without hesitation. I grabbed her face between my hands. "Mama! Mama!" Her eyes seemed to be moving independently. Drool trickled from the corner of her mouth.

"What happened?" I asked the paramedic.

"I don't know. She was like this when we got here."

A red-haired woman in a raincoat stepped forward. "I made the call," she said. "She was kind of stumbling toward the gate, which seemed kind of strange, right? And then she grabbed onto that pillar, and I came over to ask if she was okay, and her eyes just like *rolled* up and she made this like, *sound?* And then she just kind of slid down the pillar. And I ran and called security. Are you her son? I'm so sorry."

"Looks like stroke," the paramedic said, "but they'll take a closer look at the hospital."

We were pulling out of the site in the ambulance when I finally saw Dad and Teresa coming toward us around the Ontario Pavilion.

Louisa is gone when I get home, of course. So are the immediate necessities—clothes, toiletries—and the more portable major items like her laptop and our DVD player. There are three gouges in the wall across the room, above the TV. There doesn't seem to be a note. Unless you count the gouges.

Mama hung on for fifteen hours before she let go. You could hardly see her face at the end for the tape and the tubes. I stayed at the hospital. Dad checked us out of our room. I don't know where

Teresa was. When we finally left for home the picnic hamper was gone from the trunk. I didn't speak all the way back to Calgary.

Or for almost three weeks after we got back.

The smashed phone is partially visible around the edge of the TV cabinet. One gouge accounted for. When I go over to pick it up I see the second casualty: the *I Ching* Judy gave me. Its grey paper dust-jacket is torn through to reveal its bright yellow cover, a split spine, a badly mashed corner. It takes me a moment to recognize what made the third gouge. A dark rectangle. Thin shards of wood spread across the floor like entrails. I kneel behind the TV and gather the wreckage into my hands. Two sections of steps and about a quarter of the dome are still together, but otherwise it's practically unrecognizable. There are crusts of white glue where pieces have separated, or have pulled free from the base. I lift it to my face and inhale the clean scent of split oak. The auguries are plain.

I'm having trouble breathing. My body goes slack, tipping forward until my forehead touches the floor. Talon-sharp scraps of the Oratory press against my forehead, my cheeks, the bridge of my nose. There's a long, high sound I've never heard before. It's coming from me.

I did this. The thing I couldn't think about.

Maybe I should have thought about it.

A voice from the armchair says: "I've never much cared for Messiaen's attempts at bird song, actually."

But of course there's no-one there.

If this were a TV show the screen would just darken on the image of me, twisted on the floor, and maybe pick up again a couple of days later. But it isn't. The foetal curl lasts ten minutes tops, after which I get up, wipe the snot off my face. Wander into kitchen. Eat crackers from a box. Wander to bathroom. Shit. Wash hands. I still have the presence of mind to wash my hands after shitting.

Retrieve the cracker box, take it to armchair. Root under chair cushion for the remote. Find pennies & bits of popcorn, but no remote. Fling the cracker box in frustration. Watch cracker dust drift in the lamplight. Find the drift of cracker dust unaccountably sad. Sob into chair back.

Continue sobbing until tired. Probably only a matter of seconds, but it seems longer. Clear throat, wipe eyes. Notice remote on pile of newspapers against wall. Storm across room. Kick newspapers. Return to chair, turn TV on. Bounce through bits of news, children's programming, episodes of *M.A.S.H.* and *Cheers* and *Golden Girls* and eventually some movie with a really young Burt Reynolds in a cowboy hat. Every so often squirm as if in actual physical pain, because, damn it, it *feels* like actual physical pain. Utter the words "Jesus fuck." Pound edge of fist against padded chair arm.

Wake up in chair in the morning. Rub kinked neck. Make coffee. Return to chair. News. Oprah. Montel. Eventually shower. Eventually change clothes. Eventually try the phone. Eventually go out into the world. Buy milk. Walk by the river. Go to work.

One foot in front of the other.

From: judy.hu@ucalgary.ca
To: jlavoie@telco.ca
Subject: Your voice-mails

Listen, please stop leaving me messages, OK? I don't think it's a good idea to see you for a while. I mean, I feel like shit about what happened, and I'm really sorry it did, but I also feel like getting together will just make it worse, if that's possible. Fix things with your girlfriend, Jason. And stay away, at least for now.

The extent of my collapse scares the shit out of me, so I make an appointment with my GP. Part of the drill is a family history. When

I mention my cousin Neil's schizophrenia she pauses and makes a note in my file.

"Parents healthy?"

"Both dead." When I elaborate there are more pauses, more notes.

The blood pressure and whatnot are all fine, as usual. She gives me a referral to some kind of specialist. She's evasive about what kind, and I don't pin her down.

One day I come home from work and the place is practically cleaned out. Everything that was hers is gone, including furniture. I no longer have a couch, or a bed, or bookcases. My books are in a heap in the corner of the dining area. Hers are gone. Only hers. It must have taken ages to sort through them.

I assume she's at her sister's, but no-one is answering, or returning my messages.

I spend a lot of time at both keyboards—at the synth working through musical ideas, which is going strangely well, and at the computer wrestling with the libretto, which is going basically nowhere. Weird panic-shots sometimes seize me, clot my throat, burn my stomach and the backs of my arms, but I push on until they pass. They leap at me from the Louisa-emptied spaces in the apartment, from the liquor ads in my gathering stack of soft-core skin-mags, from the reflection of my eyes in the mirror.

Some nights I'm at the synth until the sun comes up, headphones on, pencil between my teeth, weaving vocal lines into complex harmonies and scribbling them onto manuscript paper. If I only had some text to go with them.

If I only had a story.

Seven

CHRISTMAS IS QUICK AND QUIET. TERESA ROASTS A TURKEY THE size of a large raccoon. I give them the latest le Carré and they give me a period-instrument recording of the Saint Matthew Passion. The kids drool green and red from the tiny candy cane each of them gets, the parenting restraints thrown wildly aside for the holidays. I skip the Christmas pudding and leave by 5:30 because I can't stand to be there. I can't stand to be anywhere.

On Boxing Day I leave a message for my manager to cancel my shifts for the week. That probably screws him badly, but I won't know because after I hang up I disconnect the phone. Then I close all the curtains. Then I unscrew all the light bulbs.

Days pass, measured by dim curtain light. Sometimes people knock on my door. Sometimes they shout.

I wander the apartment. Living room, dining area, kitchen, hall, bedroom, hall. Living room, dining area, kitchen, hall, bedroom, hall.

Flats of canned vegetables in the living room. Stack of books in the dining area, still with no shelves to put them on. Pizza boxes in the kitchen. Empty walls in the hall. Sleeping bag in the bedroom. Empty walls in the hall.

Yellow.

Vegetables in the living room. Books in the dining area. Boxes in the kitchen. Emptiness in the hall.

Yellow. Something yellow.

Sleeping bag. Empty walls.

Something significant and yellow.

Living room. Vegetables. Dining area. Books. Kitchen ...

Dining area. Yellow.

A yellow book, in the stack in the dining area. With a broken spine and a crumpled corner. The one book that isn't right where Louisa left it.

I go back, lift it from the pile. I sniff it. Paper and dust. I press it against my face, mash my nose, feel the flatness of its cover on my forehead, smooth and cool. I hold it there for a while, breathing through my mouth, then I lower it and look at it. It sure is yellow. A pure, primary yellow, like a canola field or a Cheerio box. Like the hair of the blonde people in the Saturday comic strips. It's probably the yellowest thing I own. Why do I own this wonderfully yellow object again?

Oh. Yes.

I sit on the living room floor with a pad of paper and a stubby pencil and I read the *I Ching*'s divination instructions. I don't get it at first, but I re-read them until I do.

I toss the three Chinese coins Judy gave me, check their markings, and mark a horizontal line with a break in the middle near the bottom of the page. I put a little 'o' in the break because it's a changing line. According to the instructions this means it will have specific information for me later on.

I toss the coins again, and mark an unbroken horizontal line above the broken one. I keep tossing until I've built a pattern of six lines, some broken and some solid. I unfold the chart from the back of the book and determine which hexagram I've come up with. It's called *Ku: Work on What Has Been Spoiled.*

No shit.

I flip to the part of the book that explains what *Ku* means. There are several bits of interpretation. The first bit, called *The Judgment*, begins:

Work on what has been spoiled
Has supreme success.
It furthers one to cross the great water.

That could mean pretty much anything.

Then I turn to the bits about the changing lines, the ones that provide more specific guidance. I haven't thrown any changing lines other than the first one. Its commentary says:

Six at the beginning means
Setting right what has been spoiled by the father,
If there is a son,
No blame rests upon the departed father.
Danger. In the end good fortune.

I close the book and stare at its bent yellow cover.

"Are you *shitting* me?" I say out loud.

In September of 1992 Dad drove his LTD into an abutment on the Deerfoot Trail and died instantly. He wasn't wearing a seatbelt. He always said that seat belt laws—and helmet laws, and high cigarette taxes—were government interference in people's God-given responsibility for their own well being. Still, he normally wore one. He couldn't afford the demerits. But not that day.

We didn't have a funeral. Teresa didn't want people staring at the closed coffin and imagining what was inside. Instead we had a small memorial service a couple of weeks later, after the cremation. I wrote a short electronic piece for the moment of silence—a meditative piece for church organ and toy piano, with a sample lifted from Hank Williams' *Cold, Cold Heart*, which was one of Dad's favourite songs — and Ed read something from Kahlil Gibran. The urn was cloisonné, with pink peonies and gold dragons. My idea. Too cheeky, maybe.

There was no money. The house was rented, the car was totalled, and the insurance didn't pay out because they said it was suicide. They were probably right. The weather was clear that day, the road dry, traffic light. No skid marks or other signs of a driving emergency. As far as the accident reconstruction cops could tell, he just held the pedal down and aimed for concrete.

They didn't tell that to me at the time, of course. I requested a copy of the report six months later, and was surprised when they actually sent me one. I had to agree that it looked pretty deliberate.

No-one knew why he was even on the Deerfoot that day, unless that was why. He was on his lunch break from the patio-furniture warehouse near the airport where we were both working at the time. They gave us half an hour, which wasn't enough time to go anywhere, especially anywhere you had to take the Deerfoot to get to.

People kept saying he hadn't been acting out of the ordinary that morning, or at all lately. They couldn't understand why he did it. They hadn't seen it coming.

I hadn't seen it coming either, but I think I know why he did it. Not exactly why, but near enough.

My hand had slipped that morning on the loading dock while lowering a bundle of deck chairs from a semi-trailer, and I took a chair foot under the eye. By morning break I was purple and yellow down to the cheekbone. Every time I walked past Dad he stared at it. My eye. All morning.

I don't think it was the shiner he was staring at. I think it just drew his attention back to my eyes.

The eye incident happened just a couple of months after Uncle Mark had the first and worst of his strokes, on the sixth fairway at

Glenmore. Dad was lifting a rented five-iron out of their shared bag. Uncle Mark never saw his own house again. He went straight from the links to the hospital to the nursing home.

Dad had always been kind of defined by Uncle Mark, with no doubt about who was doing the defining. With Uncle Mark withering in a wheelchair all bets were off. For the rest of the summer Dad was like an overheated engine, trying to take us to football games, or coming home with pizzas and videos, or wanting to talk about *Mom* for Christ's sake.

To strain the metaphor a little, maybe on that last morning my eyes blew his radiator cap.

Fine. Maybe that strains it a lot.

It's New Year's Eve, the eve of the millennium, the eve of my mile-stone birthday, and I'm sitting on the floor where my couch used to be eating jam from a jar with a spoon. There are big parties at Olympic Plaza and the Stampede grounds, but I'm not there. I can hear noise from the bars on Electric Avenue. I'm not there either. Miranda and her husband invited me to their place, and Sleeve said I could come to the party at his Mom and Dad's, but I'm not there either.

I'm eating jam. From a jar. With a spoon.

The TV recaps the millennium's so-far-uneventful progress across the world. Chinese performers dance on a floodlit Great Wall. Fireworks flare from the edges of the Eiffel Tower. A cross is carried by torchlight to the Mount of Olives. Giant puppets prance on Parliament Hill. Time zone by time zone the lights keep staying on, and the world gradually unclenches its ass. Monkeys jump in my head.

My throat balks at the sweetness, but I'm determined. It isn't a very big jar. The bottle of rye next to it isn't a very big bottle.

More fireworks. More jam. I tip the bottle back, wince as the harsh liquid scrapes my tongue, churns the acid in my stomach. Awe juice. *Ma*-ma called the *doc*-tor and the *doc*-tor said.

Rye dribbles onto my shirt. Another spoonful of jam. I close my eyes, squeeze them shut. Happy birthday Jason.

No more monkeys jumping on the bed.

In the new year offices reopen. Lights come on, computers hum, modems hiss and honk in greeting over functioning phone lines. Economies carry on as before, and no-one admits to having been worried. I shower and eat some dry cereal, and call my manager and apologize and take about ten minutes of shit and apologize again and then schedule some shifts.

That's all I can manage that day.

The next day I dress in clothes and go outside and ride a bus to a professional building. The man in the office that I go to has a reassuring white coat and reassuring grey temples. His desk is clean and reasonably uncluttered. The business cards in the tennis-themed holder say 'Cosmetic Surgery,' but what I'm here for is more fundamental.

"I want my eyes changed back."

"Changed back to what?"

"Back the way they were."

It's the only thing that makes sense.

It explains the missing week. It explains my eyes.

Uncle Mark changed my eyes.

I've done my research. They say the surgery didn't exist yet, in 1970. But maybe it just didn't exist officially. Maybe you could find a guy bored enough and creative enough who'd slip you in after hours, after the monotonous lid-tightenings, after the help had gone home. Someone who'd covertly rise to the challenge.

I allude to the surgery without specifying when. The doctor examines my eyes closely. "Nope, no scarring. No indication of a previous procedure of any kind."

But surely a skilled enough surgeon, I say.

"There'd still be evidence of the earlier work. Maybe not visible to everyday scrutiny, but to the trained eye, under close examination."

But if the patient had been young enough, I say. He looks puzzled. I get more specific.

"*What?*"

He stands, comes around the desk. "Mr. Lavoie, I think we're done now. If you'll excuse me, please." He opens the door.

He even pronounces my name wrong.

Of course it's preposterous. But suppose when I was born I came out looking a bit too much like Uncle Larry. No Western features at all. How far might Uncle Mark have gone to spare his family his brother's reflected shame?

Maybe I should ask Uncle Mark.

He's propped in his chair as usual, eyes half-focused, hair half-combed. I get right to it.

"Where was I for that week, Uncle Mark?"

His head lolls to one side, stretching the fragile skin across the side of his neck. I can see his pulse.

"The week after I got home from the hospital. Where was I?" I lean in closer. He smells of baby powder and urine. "Was it my eyes? Did someone change my eyes?"

The wavering male voice down the hall starts up. "OooOOOoooh, Jesus *Christ*," it cries. "Oooooh, please, be with me when I die."

A flicker on the old man's face tells me I'm right.

When he has begged enough for a carrot and some noodles the man returns to his shelter in the rough encampment on the edge of the city. He borrows a pot, waits in line for water, scrounges paper and wood-scraps for a fire. As the noodles begin to soften he hears sounds in the distance—shouts, the grumble of heavy machines, metal scraping against metal. Soon people are walking past, briskly, away from the noise, and soon after that men in uniforms appear.

The one who comes for him is young, and kind. He lets the

*man finish the half-cooked noodles and pocket the half-eaten
carrot before taking him to the truck. From the back of the truck,
as it pulls away, the man sees bulldozers approaching.*

*The lower strings play a heroic theme in the tenor range as
the truck disappears offstage.*

I crumple the page and toss it across the room with the others.

What was I thinking?

One night early in the new year Sleeve comes over with a couple of
Bond movies and a case of Big Rock. He's wearing a backward
Calgary Cannons ball-cap that doesn't quite cover the raw red patch
across his hairline—a recent home exfoliation mishap. Sleeve is
probably about five years too old to wear ball-caps backward, but
there's no point in saying so unless you have an urge to be told to
go fuck yourself.

He has brought his friend Some Call Me Tim, who wears sunglasses indoors and plays Metallica too loud through the open windows of his fifteen-year-old Camaro. He recently broke up with his
girlfriend because he was bored, and now he can't shut up about it.

"Do you believe in God?" Some Call Me Tim asks as I take his
coat.

I shoot Sleeve an exasperated look.

"I couldn't just leave him out there," he says.

Sleeve scans the living room as he hefts the beer onto the stack of newspapers I'm using as a coffee table. "Hey, the Christmas farm!" he says.

"Nativity scene," I say automatically. I haven't had the will to
undecorate.

Louisa took the good one, with the individual matte-finished
clay figures. She left me the cheesy plastic one. It's the only Christmas
decoration I have. It's set up in front of the stack of newspapers I'm
using as a TV stand.

Sleeve flops down and peers at the Scandinavian-looking holy family in the brown plastic shed. The chubby Christ-baby on blobby corn-yellow straw. The blue-gowned Mary with the uneven gold halo.

No halo on Joseph, though, for some reason. I bet the folks at the Oratory would have something to say about that.

"Joe and Ma-ry had a farm," Sleeve sings. "Ee-eye ee-eye o-o-o-o-oh."

I check the case and find three bottles already empty. Some Call Me Tim obviously drove.

"*Sleeve!*" The shock in Tim's tone surprises me a little. Sleeve looks up.

"For fuck's sake, man," Some Call Me Tim says. "It's *Jesus.*"

Sleeve just smiles.

Tim can't even shut up during the movies.

Pierce Brosnan moves cautiously down a hallway, gun in both hands, a fragment of the Bond theme on solo tympani slowly repeating, building the tension ...

"I just couldn't take it any more," Tim says. "Even the sex, you know? She'd wake me up in the morning and my stomach would churn. I mean, can't I just sleep for once?"

We send him to the liquor store four blocks over for more beer, just to give ourselves a break. The beer is going faster than Sleeve expected. I'm joining in.

Goes down easier than rye.

Tim comes back to the apartment with another case, and comes back to God as Timothy Dalton slides down a rope from a DEA helicopter. "I'm talking about *God* God, you know?" he says. "Hardassed old *Bible* God. Not some new age teddy bear God, but *God.* Like, the big fucking Dad with the leather fucking belt, right?"

Sleeve rolls across the floor to the nativity scene and starts dancing it against the carpet on its corners. "There *was* a farmer *had* a god and *Je*-sus was his *name*-oh."

"*Sleeve!*" Tim is horrified.

"Jay. Eee. Ess-you-ess. Jay. Eee. Ess-you-ess."

"*Sleeve!*"

I'm grateful for the distraction.

When we run out of Bond Some Call Me Tim flips channels and finds a Bruce Willis shoot-em-up already in progress, which he and I half watch. Sleeve is spread across the carpet on his back, eyes closed, breathing rhythmically. I set the nativity scene on his abdomen and watch it move up and down.

"What's your favourite food?" Tim asks out of nowhere as Willis slaps a fresh clip into a semi-automatic pistol. He sounds oddly earnest about it.

"Why? You want something?"

"No, no. Just what's your favourite food?"

Willis covers ten paces of open space in a running crouch as machine-gun fire splinters a wall of wooden crates behind him.

"I don't know," I say. "Ice cream, maybe. Strawberry ice cream."

"OK," Tim says, stretching his lower lip toward his quivering shot glass. The beer is long gone, but I found a half bottle of lemon-flavoured vodka that Louisa had left in the freezer. He pauses. "Place?"

I sip my tea. When the beer ran out I switched to Chinese tea. "Hmm?"

"Place. Favourite place." He takes a sip and grimaces. "I hate flavoured vodka. Hate it." He tosses it back all at once.

"Favourite place? I don't know. Never thought about it."

He nods solemnly. "OK. We'll come back to it. Music. Not yours, composer boy. Someone else's. Favourite music that isn't yours."

"Easy. Bach." Then I hesitate. "Hang on. Maybe Stravinsky. *Rite of Spring.*" I think about it for a moment. "No," I finally say. "Bach. Definitely Bach."

"Solid choice," Some Call Me Tim says. He slaps his shot glass down on the cutting board that we're using as a table. "Got a favourite place yet?"

I set my teacup next to Tim's empty glass. "Yeah, I think I do. Saint Joseph's Oratory in Montreal."

Tim clatters the lip of the bottle against the edge of his shot glass, pouring himself another shot of something he doesn't even like with the intensity of the drunk trying to look focused. "What?" he says, without looking up. Focus.

"Saint Joseph's Oratory in Montreal. Church on a hill. I was there with—I was there a few months ago. Pretty impressive."

"Excellent. Goddamn *excellent*."

"Thank you."

"No problem. So here's the deal." He rolls onto his elbows and stares at me intently. "The Big Dad in the sky offers you eternity in your church on the hill, listening to Bach and eating strawberry ice cream."

"Served by naked women," Sleeve says, apparently not sleeping after all.

"Yeah, whatever," Tim says, trying to keep his focus on whatever it is that's apparently more important than Bruce Willis swinging over a chasm on a cable. "So, do you accept?"

I think for a second. There's something not quite right about the scenario, but my beer-fogged brain can't quite pin it down. The Bach is good. The Oratory. Ice cream, certainly. Still. Something.

"No," I finally say. "No, don't think so."

Tim crawls closer on his elbows. "Why not, man? Your favourite music. Beautiful big church."

"Naked women," Sleeve shouts.

"Whatever," Tim says. "And strawberry fuckin' *ice* cream, man. All your favourite stuff. What's the problem?"

And I kind of have to think it out loud. "I'm not sure. I think it's the whole eternity thing, you know? One food, one kind of music?

All stuff that I love, sure. But after a while don't you think I'm gonna *want* some Stravinsky? Or some Hank Williams, or Devo, or a steak and fries and a slice of chocolate cake? Or a *salad* even?"

"Aha!" Some Call Me Tim slaps his hand on the floor. I seem to have walked into his trap, whatever it is. "Clever you, my clever clever friend. But not." *Slap.* "Clever." *Slap.* "Enough." *Slap.* "You think you've ducked the problem, but really you've only put it off. Because it's *eternity,* man. Thousand years, couple thousand, it doesn't matter any more. Stravinsky, Talking Heads, steak, salmon, peach-mango tofu. Give it long enough and eventually it's all just the same shit, over and over and over."

"Or what if you got the wrong stuff?" Sleeve weighs in again. "Like the food is all hotel coffee shop, or the music is all pop classical shit like that Taco Bell canon that everyone always plays—"

"Pachelbel," I say, automatically.

"—or like Donny and Marie, or—who's that guy you can't stand, Jason?"

"Schumann."

"Yeah, Schumann. Jesus, Tim, suppose Jason got *Schumann?*"

Tim glares at Sleeve. He's a testier drunk than I had realized. "That's not my fucking *point.*" He turns back to me. "It's all stuff you *want.* Paradise-level stuff. And all the variety of it you want. The *point* is"—a side-glare at Sleeve here—"are you still gonna want it after a thousand years?"

"Yeah, well," I say. "A thousand years." I lift my teacup and take a sip. "Who cares? I don't have a thousand years."

"But that's my point. What if you do? Not just a thousand years, but eternity, man. Fucking eternity."

I shake my head. "There is no eternity."

Tim grabs my shoulder, a little too hard. "How do you know?" His eyes are wide and jittery. He looks genuinely scared. "How do you fuckin' *know?*"

And it opens to me, in all its simplicity. What I already know, hiding in plain sight.

That I don't know.

That I have absolutely no idea.

"I mean—" Tim says.

"Shut up," I say, hopping up to grab the Yellow Pages.

I need to know.

I bring the Yellow Pages back in and start flipping. Tim, oddly unfazed, asks what I'm looking for.

"Travel agents."

"Oh."

He's quiet for a while, as I keep flipping.

"At one-thirty in the morning?" he finally says.

A few days later I take Aunt Jasmine to a small Chinese restaurant on the little stretch of Centre Street south of the bridge. She's wearing a lavender cardigan. She bends low over her bowl and lifts a dark knot of fried pork to her mouth with enamel chopsticks that she brought from home. I can just see the roof-edge of the ersatz Temple of Heaven over her shoulder, through the window. She chews, swallows, dabs her lips with a paper napkin.

"The last letter came from Nanjing," she says. She bends to one side and reaches into her black vinyl handbag, comes up with a bundle of envelopes tied with twine. "This is all of them. They probably won't help you." She passes them to me with both hands. I wipe my fingers and take them gently, half expecting them to crumble, to drop paper dust onto the fat noodles and glistening mushrooms below them. Silly. They're barely twenty-five years old.

So few of them. So little left.

"Anything in there we followed up as best we could. We even hired someone. His report is in there, in the brown envelope at the bottom. Three pages. How true it is we don't know, of course. He could have taken our money and made it all up, what little there is. The address is on the report, but it isn't likely that he's still there." She seems about to say more, but then she looks down abruptly and picks up her chopsticks. She rests her forearm against the table edge, the tips of her chopsticks quivering lightly in the air above her plate. "Your Uncle Kwok even went over himself, for a whole month," she says, not looking up. She takes a single noodle between her chopsticks and swirls it in a smear of sauce, around and around. "He looked everywhere he could think of. Talked to everyone he could find."

Around and around.

I take a quick look at the first couple of letters, which are in English, then skip to the report, which is in Chinese. My heart sinks. "I can't read this."

There's a long silence. Aunt Jasmine lifts the single noodle to her mouth, places it on her tongue, chews, swallows. Sits. Stares at her plate, into a past she'd found a way to put behind her until I came along. After a while she sighs and smiles at me sadly. "I'll translate it for you."

I sit with the yellow book in the kitchen in the dark and open a beer.

Setting right what has been spoiled the book says. *It furthers one to cross the great water,* it says. I take a long pull on the brown bottle. And *Danger.* And *No blame.* I like that one. No blame.

Cross the great water.

No blame.

Eight

"IT'S CALLED A POWER OF ATTORNEY, AUNT JASMINE." STATIONERY- store documents cover one end of her dining-room table, several blanks already filled with her name, in my handwriting. At the other end of the table, near the fading daylight from the kitchen door, Uncle Kwok pays us no attention as he grinds a black ink stick into the shallow depression in a grey inkstone. He adds a few drops of water with his brush from a flower-patterned saucer, then a few more, mixes the ink with the pointed tip of the bristles.

Over the course of the spring I've been getting things in order for the trip. Passport and visa and vaccinations. Intensive Mandarin lessons two evenings per week at a pricey private language school. Thank God for Eph Grant's action movie, which is still pulling in enough of an audience to keep it playing on a few suburban screens and, more to the point, to maintain a steady trickle of cash into my travel account.

"I know what a power of attorney is, Jason," Aunt Jasmine says. "I just don't know why you want to give one to me."

Uncle Kwok carefully sets the brush aside. He takes a sheet of rice paper from a stack at his elbow, positions it on the plastic place-mat before him, and weights its corners with small stones. He places the inkstone near its top edge.

"Just in case." Not really knowing in case of what. Just in case.

Uncle Kwok twirls the brush horizontally in the shallow edge of the ink, then holds it upright and makes a quick, smooth motion across the paper, left to right. A single horizontal line.

"Yes, of course, one never knows. But why come to me? You have friends, professionals, who must know more about these things."

A small grimace crosses Uncle Kwok's face. He eases the rice paper from under the stones, folds it in two, and drops it into the wicker wastebasket at his feet. He selects another sheet and positions it.

It's a good question. Sleeve would be the logical choice. Miranda, even. Yet somehow, no. "It's because you're family," I finally say, weakly. It's true, but only to a point. Past that point I can't seem to see.

Uncle Kwok makes another brisk motion, another horizontal line. Another small grimace. The second sheet follows the first into the basket.

"Fine," she says. "What do I need to do?"

Uncle Kwok tucks a third sheet under the stone weights.

"Sign here on this one, and here on this one," I say. She does, in ballpoint pen, in her tidy, legible hand.

Uncle Kwok makes another horizontal line, on the fresh sheet. He pauses and squints, then nods to himself.

"Thanks, Auntie," I say, quickly gathering the papers and getting to my feet. If traffic isn't too bad I still have time to get to the passport office before it closes.

The pocket of my jeans catches the corner of the table. It lifts, flipping Uncle Kwok's inkstone onto the page, sending a vertical black dribble across his perfect horizontal line.

He looks up. His widening eyes meet mine as the table crashes back down to the floor. I open my mouth to apologize, but before I can utter a sound he's out of his chair with a speed that I wouldn't have imagined and has slammed me against the dining room wall, his hands bunching the fabric of my shirt against my neck.

"You think we didn't try?" he says, his voice harsh and thick. He twists the fabric tighter, leans closer so that our faces are almost touching. "More than twenty years now. My own son. You think we didn't try?" His jaw trembles but his eyes are rock solid, daring me to believe for even a moment that he didn't do everything that a father could have done.

Then Aunt Jasmine quietly moves to his side and places a hand on his clenched fingers. "Let go, Kwok."

At the door Aunt Jasmine gives me her translation of the investigator's report, and I put it in a folder with my photocopies of Uncle Larry's letters. I read it all in the car—the letters for the fourth or fifth time—but they all raise more questions than they answer. I need context. I need to know how they fit into what was going on in China at the time. I still have Judy's reading list, but if I pull facts out of books on my own I'll probably just end up with a bigger pile of facts. I need to know what they mean, how they fit together. What I really need is help from Judy, which is ridiculous of course. Judy doesn't return my calls.

But maybe if I pitched it as an academic consultation. That's all it really is. We meet, she helps me out, that's it. And if there happens to be any energy there, well ... No, forget that. According to Ed she's seeing some guy from the English department who's apparently the leading *Death in Venice* scholar in western Canada or something.

I dither for a while, then leave as coolly formal a message as I can on her machine. Going to China. Have some letters. Need some context. Her call back a couple of hours later is just as formal. She agrees to meet for lunch tomorrow at a roadhouse restaurant near the campus. Not for dinner I notice, or even for a drink. Or at her office or one of our homes, God forbid.

Just as well.

I arrive a little early. The place is suitably impersonal, one of those warehouse-like suburban restaurants decorated with old farm implements and pictures of James Dean. I get a table and order a beer.

Judy is right on time. "Hey," she says as she pulls out the chair across from me. There's a polite smile on her lips, but not in her eyes. Her dark shirt is buttoned to the neck, her hair fastened back with a heavy pewter clip. She could be here to sell me a time-share or a cremation package. She looks at the beer in surprise, but doesn't say anything.

"Hey," I reply.

The server is right there. Judy just orders a soda water and an appetizer salad. I order the roast beef sandwich and another beer. A part of her *really* seems to want to ask about the beer, but apparently another part of her wants *not* to ask even more.

"So." She looks at her watch. "I have a tutorial in a little under an hour. What specifically do you want to know?" Straight to the point. And a tight schedule. She has planned this brilliantly.

I pull out the folder with the letters and the report, and hand it to her across the table. "The letters are all dated. July of '75 through February of '76. I know generally that there was a power struggle at the time between Deng and the Gang of Four, and that Deng eventually lost. What I need to know is how that fits with these specific dates. If that political context could have affected what happened to my uncle."

Judy opens the folder and reads through each document slowly. The food and drinks arrive. She sips her soda and reads each one again.

"Well," she says, her eyes on the last letter. "At least he wasn't in Beijing on April fifth. That's something." She glances at her watch, makes a little 'ooh' sound, and takes a quick forkful of salad.

"Why? What's the deal with April fifth?"

She pauses in mid-chew. "Big demonstration in Tiananmen Square that day. Kind of foreshadows the one in '89. Heads smashed. Maybe some deaths. Reports vary."

This is new to me. "What about? Some kind of anti-government protest?"

"Not exactly, though it kind of turned out that way. It was a display of public mourning for Zhou Enlai, who died three months earlier."

That doesn't make sense to me. "They smashed heads because people were in mourning for Zhou Enlai?"

Judy quickly chews another forkful of salad, her lower lip glistening appealingly with vinaigrette. "Mmm-hmm. Zhou was on the other side of the power struggle with the Gang of Four. When he died the Gang suppressed public mourning." She pauses for another forkful, then continues. "Not a great move, because the people loved Zhou. All that suppressed feeling bubbled back up at the end of March, and by April Tiananmen was filling up with wreaths and poems and thousands of people. The kind of thing your uncle would probably have wanted to be part of if he'd been in Beijing at the time."

"Yeah, sounds like."

All that suppressed feeling.

She finishes her salad and flips through the letters again. She frowns at the last of them and shakes her head. "To be honest with you Jason," she says, "I can't see that the political context is going to help you much with this." She straightens the letters and puts them back in the folder. "I mean fine, your uncle was on the wrong side of the Gang when their fortunes turned around. So were a lot of much bigger players, and your uncle had basically gotten out of Dodge by then. I doubt he was even on anyone's radar." She holds the folder toward me. "Sorry."

I don't take the folder. "No, that helps," I say quietly. "Gives me a context I didn't have before." Her little smile still doesn't reach her eyes. "Listen, those are extra copies. Why don't you hang on to them? If anything else occurs to you, let me know."

She hesitates, uncomfortable with my suggestion. "All right," she says. "Sure. I can send you an e-mail or something." She looks at her watch again. "Listen, I really have to go." She reaches into her purse. "What's my share?"

"On me. Consider it your consultant's fee."

"Thanks. That's nice of you. Well, 'bye then. Good luck in China."

And just before she dashes off to her tutorial she honest-to-God shakes my fucking hand.

There is a small farewell party at work after closing one night. A couple of pizzas, a dozen Big Rock and an Okanagan Chardonnay. The single dad will be taking over for me as acting assistant manager—I'm taking a leave of absence rather than quitting outright—and so it's a bit of a celebration of his promotion as well. It's all quite sweet. They give me a *faux* snakeskin passport case, and I give them some bullshit about discovering my heritage, and we all go home by ten.

Sleeve and Miranda are both over on my last night in Canada. It's supposed to be a leisurely farewell dinner, but I'm still frantically packing. Sleeve is running through my list of medical must-takes.

"Antibiotics?"

"Check."

"Antihistamines?"

"Check."

"Which is your most important pair of pants?" Miranda asks, looking between the layers in the big suitcase.

"Laxative?"

"Check. Depends. What do you mean by 'most important'?"

She lifts two flattened flannel shirts with one palm and with the other lifts a corner of the khakis beneath. "Most significant. Most useful."

"Anti-diarrhoea medicine?"

"Check, two kinds. Most useful how, exactly?"

She peers at the jeans under the khakis. "Say you end up down to one pair. Which pair is it?"

"Disinfectant ointment?"

"That pair. The jeans. Check."

Miranda slides out the jeans without disturbing the surrounding items. She folds back the waistband and takes a thick pen from her purse.

"What's that?"

"Laundry marker." She pulls off the cap with her teeth.

"Hey. What're you doing?" I lean across, but she slaps my hand away.

"You're getting a phone number where you won't lose it," she mumbles around the pen-cap. She starts writing on the inside of the waistband in big, boxy characters. "E-mail address too."

"OK, come on," Sleeve says. "We're nearly done here and I'm starving. Disinfectant wipes?"

Miranda's printing, made slow and childlike by the awkward marker, works its way around the inside edge of my pants.

"Yeah," I say. "Check."

I stop at a Grand and Toy and use their self-serve copier to make an extra set of Uncle Larry's letters and the investigator's report. I buy a red binder, a set of write-on tabbed dividers, four different-coloured highlighters and a three-hole punch. Then I go to a travel book store, where I pick up a Lonely Planet guide to China and detailed maps of Beijing and Nanjing.

I check my e-mail at an internet cafe and to my surprise find a message from Judy. I feel a twinge of excitement as I open it, but it's just an impersonal—though wonderfully detailed—context-memo about Uncle Larry's letters. Nothing new, just a print version of what she said at the roadhouse. Nice of her to go to the trouble. I print two copies.

That evening I spread everything on the living room floor, put my *erhu* CD on, and open a beer. I hole-punch the letters, the report, and Judy's e-mail and put them in the binder. I write the date of each letter and the names of the other two documents on the corresponding divider tabs. The *erhu* CD ends, so I put on the CBC CD with my string trio and open another beer.

I sit with my back against the living room wall and go through the documents one by one, highlighting places in blue, people in green, events of political significance in pink. I keep yellow in reserve, in case I come up with anything else that I need to flag. I change the CD again—Stravinsky's *Rite of Spring* this time—and open another beer.

I unfold the maps and locate the places referred to in the documents. I highlight them in blue, and make a note next to each one in black pen explaining its significance. Where the location relates to a particular person or political event I highlight the note in green or pink.

I decide to include on the maps a series of little notes cross-referencing each location to the relevant document. I highlight those in yellow. I knew I'd need it. I make corresponding margin notes on each document, with the grid-locations of the relevant spots on the map. Philip Glass and another beer. In a glass. Because that seems funny to me.

I spread the maps on the floor and squat between them, turning my head from one to the other with my eyes half-focused, half hoping to see a pattern in the little blocks of pink or green, or of all of the colours together.

Nothing.

Maybe if I worked out a way to plot them chronologically.

The cab lets me out at the airport and I tip the driver heavily because I'm trying to shed the last of my Canadian money. I keep enough for coffee. I try to sling the duffel bag over my shoulder but my backpack is in the way, so I carry it by the hand loops to the check in.

The counter clerk is harried but pleasant. "Now you know you'll have to claim the bags in Vancouver and then check them through again for Beijing?" she says as she lifts the backpack onto the conveyor belt with both hands. I tell her I know. I take my boarding pass and my small carry-on—a green army surplus shoulder pouch with my notebook, phrase book, the *I Ching* Judy gave me, two apples, two pens, a thick paperback thriller set in Shanghai, and my binder with the photocopies of Uncle Larry's letters—and head toward the gate. On my way I get a coffee and a copy of the *Herald*. It's about forty-five minutes to flight time.

I find a seat near the gate with a view of the tarmac and open my paper. Near the window a noisily excited five-year-old bounces beside his mother. "Mommy look," he says. "It's the landing gear. Look, Mommy, that's the landing gear." No response. "Look, Mommy, another airplane is landing. A blue one. Look, Mommy."

His mother just sits, blank-faced.

According to Aunt Jasmine they made three official inquiries about Uncle Larry through External Affairs in Ottawa, in June and September of 1976 and February of 1977. Each time they received an inconclusive reply three to five months later.

In January of 1977 they hired a friend of a friend in Nanjing to look for Uncle Larry. They received interim reports in April, July and October of 1977, which basically just said that the investigator was following some leads but needed more time and money. So they kept sending him money. When they finally stopped and insisted on seeing some results he sent them a final report in January of 1978. It didn't add much to what they already knew.

There are a few things in it I intend to follow up on, though.

When Aunt Jasmine and Uncle Kwok realized the investigator wasn't going to find their son, Uncle Kwok went over. He spent most of the summer of 1978 going where the investigator had gone and wherever else he could think of, but without any luck. Uncle Larry had vanished.

The five-year-old has discovered the safety card, and is loudly providing stories for the pictograms. "See Mommy, they know the plane is going in the water, and then after they go here, and then the man sees a fire, see Mommy? See, first they know the plane is going in the water ..."

I reach under the seat for my carry-on and pull out the binder. The first letter, at Tab 1, is dated July 30, 1975.

Dear Mother and Father:

I have arrived in Beijing, and as planned I am staying with my friend Wei. Things are quite chaotic here. There is a lot of talk about the Four Modernizations, but even though they must need skilled people I haven't met anyone yet who can tell me how to go about finding actual engineering work. Wei doesn't know anyone who can help, as his interests are more strictly political.

While I get settled and look around I am helping Wei with a small newspaper that he and some friends of his publish every few weeks in support of the new reforms. He's been keen to have it translated into English for distribution in areas where there are foreigners, so to him my arrival here is a blessing.

Some of Wei's more cautious friends say he should temper his enthusiasm for the new reforms, that political tides here have a way of shifting, but he insists that this time Deng and Zhou have such momentum that there can be no turning back. And I believe he's right. This is exactly what I had hoped to be a part of, and now I am (or at least I will be as soon as I find a position where my skills can be put to use).

With respect,
Your son, Lihuang

At the bottom he provides a return address, presumably Wei's.

As I understand it from Judy, there were still serious political tensions at that point between the modernizers and the old Cultural Revolution crowd, and those tensions came to be personified in Deng and Madam Mao, with Mao favouring one or the other at different times. Wei's friends were right to be cautious.

I've marked the address on my map of Beijing, in the pocket of my binder. It's near the Temple of Heaven. Louisa would probably see something auspicious in that. I appreciate that I'm not likely to find anything there after twenty-five years, especially since Uncle Kwok checked the neighbourhood himself only three years later. But I want to be thorough, and I have to lay over in Beijing anyhow.

The nine-hour flight gives me plenty of time to go through the binder, work through some Mandarin exercises in the phrase book, read about a third of the thriller, and catch a few non-consecutive hours of restless sleep. By the time we stop for fuel in Shanghai I'm dazed and foggy, and by the time we lift off again for Beijing all I can think about is the straight line from where I am now to the dark safety of hotel bedcovers. This was a crazy, stupid thing to do. Talk about overreacting to a breakup.

Landing, line-ups, customs, cab stands. Nothing registers with me but the straight line. I have achieved one-pointed consciousness.

I'm booked into a high-end hotel not far off of Chang-an. It's walking distance from Tiananmen Square in an area bounded by grey walled *hutong* dwellings and a multi-level shopping complex. Without a clear sense of the customs or the currency I apparently overtip the cab driver lavishly, judging by the way his eyes widen and by the enthusiasm with which he hauls my bags to the brass and velvet luggage cart that two smiling bellmen are wheeling to the curb. The counter staff speak English, so the formalities are brief and my shivering fatigued-to-the-core body is knees-to-chest under a duvet by what feels to it like five thirty in the morning.

It doesn't wake again for fifteen hours.

I gradually surface into unfamiliar street sounds and a slice of sun-light between dark curtains. I lie there in stunned semi-disbelief that I've actually done this, that I'm actually in China, until a few strands of will braid together and lift me out of the covers. I unpack (finally), shower (finally), iron a collared cotton shirt and a pair of khakis, and head down to the hotel's breakfast buffet.

The buffet is a wild collision of east and west. Scrambled eggs and crisp bacon next to a kind of rice porridge called congee with side dishes of savoury toppings.[9] Cheese danishes next to steamed buns stuffed with sweet bean paste. Cold cuts and cubed cheddar next to spherical, acorn-sized mushrooms in a slippery pale sauce. Each steam tray is kept filled and tidy by a team of small men in red dinner jackets, and each is fronted by an elegant folded card ex-plaining exactly what it is in both English and Chinese.

I'm ravenous. I order an omelette with the works at the omelette bar, and while it's being made I fill a plate with blueberry pancakes and sausages. When it's empty I fill it again. I have two glasses of orange juice and three cups of coffee. My only concession to the notional left side of the Macleod Trail restaurant menu is the start-ling cup of congee.[10]

I pick up one of Beijing's red bumper-car-sized cabs on Chang-an and ask the driver to take me to the Temple of Heaven. By the time we get there my buttocks and thighs are stiff from clenching. When he turns down the east side of Tiananmen Square he fits the cab in front of a tour bus with less than a foot to spare, while a truck com-ing the other way fits just as tightly in front of us, everyone simply adjusting to everyone else as they go. The whole ride is like that.

---

9. I learn this by topping mine with what I think is brown sugar, but which turns out to be like a salty, crumbled dried fish or something.
10. Ibid.

When we arrive at the Temple I try to tip him with a U.S. dollar, but he nervously refuses to take it.

Wei's twenty-five-year-old address is still there, but at this point it's a noodle shop at street level and an herbalist above. I show Uncle Larry's picture to anyone within the block who looks older than forty, but the only reactions I get are either blank stares or puzzled inquiries—accompanied by glances back and forth from the picture to my face—about what happened to my eyes or why my Chinese is so bad.

This first stage of my investigations takes under an hour, and yields exactly nothing other than a bowl of noodles in broth and a decent oolong tea.

Yeah, well. What was I expecting?

Since the Temple of Heaven is right across the road I pay the nominal entry fee and enter the complex. It's a sprawling park filled with specialized ceremonial buildings, some of them linked by a broad processional causeway. I follow the causeway to the building Calgary's cultural centre is modelled on, the Hall of Prayer for Good Harvests. It has a three-level roof rather than the single level in Calgary, but otherwise I'm impressed by the resemblance: the blue tiles, the red roof-edge, the gold bauble on top. I climb the concentric stone platforms that surround the Hall and go inside.

My eye is drawn immediately upward, even more than in the truncated Calgary version. The layered ceiling is even more intricate and colourful, flaring farther out and down in half a dozen additional rings of ornamentation. The complexity of it is overwhelming. When I focus on the details I lose any sense of the whole, and when I try to take in the whole I lose the details. It takes me some time to relax into it, to open to the whole *as* the details. Columns above columns. Repeated patterns of lotuses, dragons, phoenixes and floral images in blues and greens and gold leaf. At the apex, a glorious gold spiral dragon surrounded by scarlet rectangles framed in gold-edged green.

I stand, staring, my breath slow and deep, stunned by the bare existence of this space where centuries of collective yearning have been channelled every spring through emperor after emperor in elaborate ceremony. The hall in Calgary, built only a few years ago by people who look like me, replicates this building, built over a hundred years ago by people who looked like me, which replicates the five-hundred-year-old temple that was destroyed by fire, also built by people who looked like me. One direct line. For a moment as I stand here, staring up, I see the Calgary temple as an overlay, its subtle differences shimmering around this temple in Beijing.

But I can't hold on to it. It slides sideways and is gone.

PART III

Nine

THE CHECK-IN CLERK AT THE BEIJING AIRPORT TELLS ME — IN English—that I have too much luggage for the flight to Nanjing. I can take only one bag, and it has a weight limit. With a grunt and a scowl I lift my duffel bag back onto the wire cart and push it toward a nearby bench.

It takes me about ten minutes to cull my clothes to what will fit into my backpack. Into the duffel bag go my dress shoes and blazer, my fleece-lined windbreaker, three shirts, two pairs of pants, about half of my socks and underwear, and most of my bulkier books. I lock the duffel bag in a locker and get back into line.

The backpack meets the weight limit, and the clerk checks me through.

The flight is short and uneventful. As I leave the plane in Nanjing the flight attendant gives each passenger a shiny brass key ring with the carrier's logo on it, a reward for choosing to fly with them. Apparently China's air market is getting competitive. I clip it to the zipper on my backpack.

Outside the Nanjing terminal are a couple of two-story-high inflatable dolls, round-faced stylized children in colourful hats, mascots for some local festival. I wait in their shadow for the bus into the city. The bus ride takes twenty minutes.

I check into my hotel, unpack and iron my clothes, hang them in the closet, and then make a cup of tea, stretch out on the bed and get out my binder. I flip to the investigator's report.

The report confirms that Larry had worked at the Nanjing Museum, but says that the museum doesn't have an address for him.

Hey, I have to start somewhere.

I put on my light jacket and hiking shoes, pack my binder and some pencils into my satchel and have a look at my map. The Nanjing Museum isn't far from the Zhongshan Gate. I head to the desk and they call me a cab.

The cab drops me beside a football-field-sized garden framed by broad, low buildings with upturned roof corners. This is the museum: not a single building, but a complex of gardens and lakes, and eleven separate exhibition halls.

That'll be a lot of staff, I think.

And for the first time I get a gut sense of the size of my task.

How, in this complex, am I going to find someone who remembers one guy, twenty-five years ago? How in this *country?* The sheer idea of it pins me where I am, on a Nanjing roadside ten time-zones from home in a country of a billion faces. All of these buildings, these streets. These *lives.* What was I thinking? Uncle Kwok was here when the trail was fresh, and he came up with zip. How could I think I could do better all these years later? How do I even try?

The weight of it won't let me stand. I sit on the grass, cross-legged, my arms holding my satchel against my chest.

How do I even try?

For a while—I have no idea how long—I just sit there, elbows on knees, damp grass cold through my jeans. *How do I try?* Then almost as if to spite myself, to prove to myself that there is no answer, looking for what should have warned me away from this wasted trip in the first place if I'd only been paying attention, I take out my binder and flip through it angrily, all but ripping the margin holes. Page after page of the bullshit I've followed here so blindly, the pointless incidents in banal letters home, the half-assed observations cooked up into worthless reports. Each piece so tiny, so tiny on its own. God *damn* it.

I rip out a handful of pages and crumple them and hold them against my face, stifling a howl.

So tiny and pointless.

Each piece. So fucking tiny.

"On its own," a voice behind my shoulder says.

I turn sharply to see who it is.

There's no-one there. Not even nearby. Just open space.

Did I really hear it?

I look down at the binder, at the pages in the binder, at the dozens of them. At the accumulation of them.

Each piece so tiny.

On its own, I hear again, this time in my head. For sure.

Thank Christ, I think.

I draw a long breath through crumpled foolscap, and let it out again.

I put the crumpled pages down and smooth them with my hands as best I can. I fit the torn edges of the holes back around the binder rings. I take another long breath.

Close the binder. Place it gently into the satchel. Rub my eyes with the heels of my hands. Run my palms up across my forehead, my fingertips through my hair and across my scalp.

How can I try?

Well not by sitting in the grass on the roadside, that's for damn sure.

I cross the garden and climb a set of broad steps to the large, red-pillared building that appears to be the main hall and ask a young woman behind a counter whom I can speak to about a former employee.

The woman makes a phone call. She's on the line for some time. After a few minutes she cups her palm over the mouthpiece and suggests that I have a seat.

After a while the phone call ends, and a while after that a functionary in a dark business suit appears through a door. He shakes my hand and introduces himself. He doesn't smile. He is probably in his forties, with shallow-set eyes and almost wrinkleless skin.

He leads me to a quiet courtyard with tidy lawns and a broad gravel path, and we sit on a wooden bench under a tile-roofed colonnade. We have the courtyard to ourselves apart from a grey-haired gardener in blue coveralls. The gardener glances up as we enter, then goes back to delicately pruning a low bush with a pair of iron shears.

"So," the functionary says. "You have an inquiry about a former employee?"

I take out Larry's picture. "My uncle," I say. "I believe he worked here, in 1976. Translating brochures and things into English."

The man takes the picture and studies it carefully. He's posturing. He would've been a teenager in 1976. He keeps his gaze on the picture for a suitable length of time before he responds. Maybe even actually counting the seconds. "I'm sorry," he finally says, "but we do not provide information to the public about our employees. Present or past. It's a question of privacy."

I nod. "I understand. But not even to family?"

He spreads his hands. "How would I know you are family?"

I take the picture back and hold it up beside my face.

"Even so," he says.

He rises to go, and produces a pass and a folded map from his breast pocket. "I'm sorry I can't help you," he says, "but please feel free to stay and see the museum. Our collection of paintings and calligraphy is particularly extensive. Westerners are also often interested in the exhibit dealing with the Taiping Heavenly Kingdom Revolution. You'll find it on the map."

And he walks elegantly across the gravel to a doorway, and disappears.

Well, fuck you.

I unfold the map. It gives me the general layout of the place. Each building, each exhibit room. I assume the unlabelled rooms are staff only. So those are the ones I start with.

I wait by a locked door with frosted glass and quietly approach anyone with grey hair who comes through. There aren't many. I manage to speak to two older women before an officious man about my age in a black blazer says I should leave or he'll call security. No-one recognizes the man in the photo. Or at least no-one admits to it.

I repeat the process at three more locked doors in two more buildings, with the same result.

My luck is no better with the staff in the public areas. Guides, guards, gift shop staff. Most are too young, and those who are old enough are too new to the museum.

Eventually I finish up in the same courtyard where the functionary left me earlier in the day. The light is fading, but the grey-haired gardener is still there. Now he's edging the grass along the flower beds. He looks up, and peers at me curiously.

What the hell. He's old enough.

His clothes smell of tobacco, his iron shears of mineral oil and crushed leaves.

"You were here earlier," he says. "Speaking with the man in the suit."

I can only just understand him. His dialect is quite different.

"Yes. Yes, I was."

"You showed him a picture."

"Yes."

"You look familiar to me. Will you show me the picture?"

I don't hesitate.

"I know this man," the gardener says. "The family name is Po, am I right?"

I feel a tiny adrenaline surge.

I nod. "Po Lihuang. My uncle."

He nods too, slowly. "Yes. He worked in the office here. American, I think. I didn't know him well, but he was always filled with enthusiasm." He lowers his voice slightly. "At a time when that was something that most people took care not to show."

It's all I can do to keep my voice steady. "Do you know where he is now?"

He frowns and waves a dismissive hand. "No, no. Of course not. It was many years ago. Many years." He looks away, a little agitated.

I drop my voice, keeping my tone as calm as I can. "I understand." I touch his shoulder lightly. "Look at me. Please look at me," I say, and after a moment he does. His eyes are grey and tired, and slightly wary. "Is there anything at all that you can tell me about him, about that time?"

He looks directly into my eyes for a long moment, deciding. Then he decides.

"He lived in the Confucius Temple area. I'm pretty sure that's where it was."

I pull out my binder and open it to a fresh page. "Confucius Temple," I say, writing it down. "Do you know exactly where?"

"No, no. I never went there."

"Anything? Was it a house, an apartment?"

The gardener shakes his head. "I didn't know him well."

It isn't much, but it's more than I'd expected.

"Thanks," I say, touching the old man's shoulder again.

But he isn't done.

"I didn't know him well," he says, "but he was friends with Ah Xiang. He and Ah Xiang often sat together in this garden."

"Ah Xiang?" I write it down. "Do you know what they talked about?"

"No, no. I never asked."

I lean in towards him, almost afraid to ask. "And is Ah Xiang still alive?"

He nods. "He fixes bicycles, near the Zhonghua Gate."

Sparks jump up my spine. The investigator spoke to someone at a bike factory. It's in his report. He got a few bits of information before the man grew suspicions and refused to say more. According to this man Larry received a visit from a friend of his from Beijing in early 1976, just before he left the museum.

But in one of its many failings, the report describes the building that the bike factory was in but doesn't provide the address.

I note the name *Ah Xiang* and the area in my binder.

"Thanks again," I say. "Thanks very much."

"Or at least he used to," the old man says, almost to himself, as he bends toward the bush again with his iron shears.

Over dinner in the hotel dining room I spread my binder and map across a table for four and go over what I have. I'm two tiny pieces further ahead, but a lot will depend on where they lead, if anywhere.

Ah Xiang sounds like the better bet—a name rather than a neighbourhood—but the gardener only had a vague sense of where the bike repair shop was. At least the Confucius Temple area is clearly marked on my map. I decide to make that my first stop tomorrow.

Before I go back to my room I stop at the hotel gift shop for something to read, since most of my books are in an airport locker in Beijing. They don't have much in English, but what they do have includes a slim abridgement of *Journey to the West*, the epic that Judy ended up never lending to me.

"Monkey King," the clerk says. "A well-known figure in Chinese folklore."

At eight the next morning I call Aunt Jasmine, timing my call for the Calgary dinner hour in the hope of catching her at home. I do.

"Jason. What a nice surprise. Where are you?"

We go through the usual necessary preliminaries, and then I ask her about Confucius Temple and the bike shop.

There is a reflective pause. "No-o," she says slowly. "I don't remember anything about those places. Just a moment." I hear her call out to Uncle Kwok, and there's a short exchange I can't make out. Then she comes back.

"Your uncle says that he did speak to someone at a bicycle factory in Nanjing, and that a man who knew Lihuang had worked there, but he was gone. No-one could tell your uncle where." She sighs. "I'm sorry."

"Don't worry about it," I say. "Does he remember the address where the bike factory was?"

She calls out to him again, and when she comes back on she sighs.

"He says 'no.' Only the neighbourhood. It was near the Zhonghua Gate."

Damn. I was counting on more. Like an actual address.

On the other hand at least it corroborates the gardener. Maybe that's something.

The Confucius Temple area is a narrow-laned warren of restaurants, food stalls, and shops crammed with painted bottles, jade pendants, lacquer ware, enamelled vases, framed calligraphy, embroidered silk clothes, folding fans, chopsticks, scrolls, and mass-produced statuettes of lions, dragons, dogs, pigs, snakes, horses, roosters and rabbits, fat smiling Buddhas and lean Taoist Immortals. I move from shop to stall to shop. Wherever I see someone who looks old enough to have been there twenty-five years ago I show them Larry's picture. I do this for two days. I speak to everyone I can find.

No-one recognizes him. Though I get a couple of puzzled questions about my eyes.

By the end of the second day my museum roadside enthusiasm

is spent. This is pointless. I'm disheartened and hungry and my legs ache and I deserve a treat, so I go into an upscale restaurant with window tables overlooking a lagoon and order a multi-course banquet—clear soup, sticky rice, barbecued pork, stir-fried greens, pressed duck, and a couple of bottles of *Tsingdao*. During the soup course I see one of the kitchen staff peering at me through a round window in a steel swinging door, a man a little older than I am, with close-cut hair and thick-rimmed glasses.

Spot the Westerner. I'm a curiosity everywhere I go.

A little later, as I dip the edge of the last slice of pork into a dish of hot sauce, I see him there again, looking at me. Looking puzzled.

Enjoy the show.

And when the jacketed server brings my change and I get up to leave, the man from the kitchen comes through the swinging door and over to my table.

Well, he is kitchen staff. "It was very nice," I say. "Thank you."

It's as though he doesn't hear me. "I think I must know you," he says in English, "but I don't think it can be."

This makes me pause.

"Why would you know me?"

His eyes are intent and serious behind his glasses. "I think you lived near our family's work group, many years ago. But you are too young. I must be mistaken."

I take Larry's picture from my jacket. "Is this who you think I am?"

He holds it close to his face, looks up at me, then nods his head. "Yes, I see. Your eyes are different. This is your father?"

I shake my head. "My uncle."

He looks back at the photo. "He used to have tea with my father. I was a boy. They would sit in our courtyard in the mornings before this man went to his work at the restaurant, and my father would give him tea and they would look at the newspapers together."

My heart sinks a little.

"Restaurant? No, that can't be right. He worked at the museum."

His face brightens, another piece of memory clicking into place. "Yes, of course. The museum. He was at the museum at first, but he left it to work at the restaurant."

That doesn't make sense. I knew from the investigator's report that Larry left the museum, but why would he move from a decent job like that to work in a restaurant? Could the friend from Beijing have had a better job for him there? But then why wasn't the job *in* Beijing? And how would a restaurant job be better than doing translations for the museum? Another tiny piece, but it doesn't fit well.

"Do you know which restaurant? Was it here, in Confucius Temple?"

He lowers the photo and stares into the middle distance, frowning in thought. "No, not here. He had to travel. A long walk. Near the mausoleum, I think."

"The mausoleum?"

He looks at me in surprise. "You don't know the mausoleum?" He can't believe my ignorance. I shake my head. "Where Doctor Sun is buried," he says, his voice reverential. "On the mountainside."

The next morning I take a cab to the mausoleum site, but as it climbs the well-paved road from parking lot to parking lot I see that it's a huge complex of booths, shops, teahouses, restaurants and educational facilities. *All that staff.* I feel the same sense of enormity that I felt on the museum roadside, but I try to hold it down.

At least it's only the restaurants.

But which one?

I have the driver drop me near a broad walkway and I pick up an English guidebook from a stall. As I collect my change and turn back I spot the mausoleum itself and stop dead.

Jesus God.

My first thought is that no-one in Canada could ever be buried in this kind of grandeur. Not the richest railway baron or the noblest Father of Confederation or the scrappiest high-scoring defenseman. We don't do personal commemoration on this scale. It's unseemly.

But they damn sure did it here.

A grand marble memorial arch maybe ten metres high opens onto a tree-lined promenade at least thirty metres wide and the length of several football fields. There are gift stalls along both sides, and at its other end is a massive and daunting staircase up the mountainside. Three hundred and ninety-two steps, according to the guidebook. One step for each million Chinese at the time.

I check my watch. It's early. I have plenty of time. I can afford to make the climb.

The stairs proceed in stages, separated by further memorial structures. The last set of steps is divided down the middle by a broad floral display. I'm reminded of the steps to the Oratory, divided by the pilgrims' kneeling lane. There it's penitents. Here it's flowers.

Even without a kneeling lane I'm feeling pretty penitential by the time I get to the top. To Dr. Sun's memory I offer my sticky-dry mouth and the shooting pain in my calves. Thankfully there's a cart selling bottled water, and a shaded bench where I can sit.

I wipe my face on my sleeve, undo my shoelaces and take a long pull on the bottle, swirling the cool water in my mouth before I swallow. It's better than beer. I take another pull, then recap the bottle and roll it along my forehead.

The area in front of the tomb is crowded with decorous couples and small families, and a handful of western tourists, sticking out like fattened geese. I sit in the shade and watch them come and go —the grey-haired couple in the matching Hawaiian shirts, the blond man with the blond eyebrows, the tanned young couple with their hands wedged into each other's back pockets. The locals take it all in slowly, even reverentially. The westerners are in the tomb for maybe three minutes each. *I'll take a picture of you, then you take a picture of me. Oh, and get the inscription on the wall while we're at it.* You can almost see them ticking Dr. Sun off their list as they leave.

All but the blond man. I sip my water for a good half hour after he goes into the tomb, but he doesn't come back out.

I work my way through the restaurants. I get some comments on my resemblance to the photo, but apart from that, nothing.

At the last and largest place, a tearoom and gift shop, it takes me a while to find someone to speak to because the staff are all busy seating a busload of middle-aged white couples with Chinese babies. There seems to be a shortage of high chairs—and in particular of high chairs that a couple of the women feel are sufficiently safe—and every second regular chair seems to be occupied by a fat canvas diaper bag. Six or eight white-coated servers mill about arranging seating, taking drink orders, distributing tureens of thick soup and two-litre bottles of orange pop. Then they vanish, leaving me standing there with a youngish man who seems to be the group's guide and translator. He gives me an apologetic look.

"Sorry," he says in English. "We kind of take a place over when we arrive."

At almost every table new parents balance babies on knees, mix Pablum with boiled water from thermoses, blow on flat spoonfuls of soup until they're tepid enough for tiny lips. Babies squirm or doze or lean into each spoonful of food like it was their last. No-one is paying the slightest attention to us.

"How did you know I spoke English?"

The guide grins, pleased at being right but trying not to let on. "Pretty obvious. If you want to eat you might have to wait a bit. Unless you want to join us? I could tell them you're my cousin or something."

"No, no, thanks. I just need to speak to the staff. I'm looking for someone who I think used to work here."

"Oh yes? Who?"

This strikes me as a little pushy, but it's no secret, so I show him Larry's picture.

"But this is you," he says, puzzled.

"No, it's my uncle. See the eyes." I point. He looks at the photo, then at me.

"Ah, I see. He's about your age, though."

"At the time, yes. This picture was taken in the 70s."

He looks at it again. "Hmm. This is the last picture that you have?"

"Yes. He came here from Canada around then, and vanished."

"And you hope to find him now? Do you think that that's realistic?"

"Probably not. But I have to try."

"Why, after so long?"

"Um." What's the short answer? "Family reasons," I finally say.

"Ah." He gives me a slightly sympathetic look. Whatever he's assuming, I can't be bothered to clear it up. Not his business.

And then he surprises me. "Listen, if it was that long ago it will only be someone quite old who might remember him. Let me ask for you. The families are settled now, and I may have more luck than you because I'm from here. Older people may not trust strangers so much." He gives me a *you know how it is* look.

Off he goes to the kitchen, with his off-kilter assumptions and my photo of Larry. On his way he catches a young server by the sleeve and gestures in my direction, and she brings me a mug of tea. I sit on a chair in the entryway, out of view, and wait.

Twenty minutes later he comes back with the photo, and probably still with his assumptions, but with no new information.

"I'm sorry, but no-one here knows this person. One of them pointed to you, but the rest just said no."

"Thanks. You've been really helpful. Is there a later shift I could check with?"

"I thought that you might ask that, so I checked. There's just the one shift, all day. Anyone who isn't working today is too young to be of help. Again, I'm sorry."

So am I, but I don't say so.

Because that just leaves the bike shop.

And no-one seems to know where the bike shop is.

It takes me almost three days to find it. The gardener and Uncle Kwok have only narrowed it to a neighbourhood, and the building description from the investigator hasn't narrowed it much further, but after a virtual house-to-house I eventually get there.

I actually miss it at first, and only come back to it the following day when there's nowhere else possible left. It seems to have changed for the worse in the twenty-five years since the investigator saw it. Patchy grass grows through cracks in the pavement, around twigs and leaves and fragments of roof-tile. A broken window is covered by makeshift shutters made of mismatched planks. The door-frame leans badly to the left. It has no sign. But it's the only building in the neighbourhood that comes close to matching the investigator's description.

The room is lit by a single bare bulb hanging from the ceiling. A wrinkled man in a Mao jacket and a Nike ball cap is seated at a trestle table, rinsing ball bearings in a rice bowl of what smells like paint thinner. He looks up warily as I enter.

"May I help you?"

I bow slightly. "Excuse me," I say. "Am I addressing Ah Xiang?"

His wary eyes stay on me. "I am Ah Xiang, yes. May I help you in some way?" He lifts his fingers from the rice bowl and wipes them on a rag.

Jesus God, I've found him. I start to tremble.

I step toward the table, into the light of the bulb. His expression changes slightly. A flicker of recognition. My pulse quickens.

He thought I was Larry. Just for a second. Just until he realized I couldn't be.

I take the photo from my pocket. "I think you know this man. My uncle. Po Lihuang. You may know him as Larry."

He wipes his fingers a second time before reaching for the photo. He takes it from me gently and holds it close to his face. The wary eyes soften. He looks up at me, then at the photo, then at me.

"Only the eyes," he says. "Otherwise you are very much like him." He scowls, thinking. "Not a nephew, though. If I remember, he has no brothers or sisters."

I smile. "You do remember. I've always called him 'uncle,' but my mother was his cousin."

"Was? Lihuang is dead?"

My stomach sinks. He doesn't know. He's asking me the thing that I was hoping he could tell me.

"No," I say. "I mean, I don't know. I meant my mother. My mother is dead."

"Oh! I'm very sorry." He looks saddened. "Dear me."

"Thank you," I say. "But she died almost fifteen years ago."

It startles me to say it out loud. That long.

"Are you looking for Lihuang then? Is that why you're here, with this picture?" He takes a last look at it before handing it back to me.

"Yes." I take the picture, but instead of putting it back into my pocket I set it gently on the table, turned toward him. Let him keep seeing it. Keep seeing the resemblance.

He pauses for a moment. "You aren't the first to come here looking for him. It has been quite a while, though."

"Nineteen seventy-eight. Two men. You told the first one you knew Lihuang from the museum, and that in 1976 he had a visitor from Beijing and left the museum. The second one was told that you no longer worked here."

"I told him that. I didn't trust him. He looked like Public Security."

I almost laugh. Sad, quiet Uncle Kwok, Public Security? Who could possibly —

Then I stop.

I was five. What can I possibly know about what he was like before, in his element, with other adults? What he was like when he was searching the streets of China for his son? Before year after helpless year of not knowing wore him down to a husk at the end of an ink brush?

I wonder whether or not to tell Ah Xiang. I almost decide not to, but it feels wrong. Part of it is that I want to be honest with him, but part of it is more calculated. If he knows he refused Larry's father, he might be more likely to help me.

"He was my uncle, actually," I say. "Lihuang's father."

His head jerks up, his mouth round with surprise. His hands drop limply into his lap. "Oh my," he says softly. "That's what he said. I didn't believe him."

He shakes his head slowly.

"His father. Oh my. And I wouldn't even speak to him. That poor, poor man." The edges of his eyes glisten.

Well, don't I feel like a shit?

Ah Xiang finds me a chair and pours two small cups of tea from a pot on the back counter. I bow in thanks and we settle into our chairs.

"So when did you start working here?" I ask. "Right after the museum?"

Ah Xiang blows across the surface of his tea. "I've always worked here," he says. "Ever since I was a boy." He takes a sip, lowers the cup. "The museum, that was extra. A way to ... to help recover what we could."

I set my teacup on the table and lean forward, my elbows on my knees. "After the Cultural Revolution?"

He pauses, then nods almost imperceptibly. A habit of silence.

But something doesn't quite make sense. "You've had a repair shop here since you were a boy?" I ask.

Ah Xiang smiles and shakes his head. "No, the repair shop only in recent years. This was once a bicycle *factory*. Our work group was the most productive in Jiangsu province. Back there"—he gestures through the opening at the back of the shop, where a warehouse-sized space with black-painted windows sits empty, apart from a neatly-folded sleeping mat and a makeshift brick fire pit with a black-ened grill—"we did almost everything. Tapped the bolts, milled the gears, cut spokes from rolls of thick steel wire. The only things that came from somewhere else were the chains and the seats, and ..." He frowns for a moment, straining to pull another detail loose, a rock wedged in a drought-hardened field. "And the tires," he says finally. "A work group near the river made the tires and tubes."

"What happened to the factory?"

"Prosperity," he says with a small smile. "Bicycles are made in Special Economic Zones now. I could work there too, I suppose. Fasten-ing two thousand seats onto two thousand seat-posts each day. But I stay here. There is still plenty to do. May I work while we talk?"

"Yes, of course."

He picks a bearing from the bowl, wipes it with a clean rag, in-spects it carefully, and places it on a bamboo mat on his work surface. "My usual job was cutting and welding steel pipe into frames, though we all knew how to do a bit of everything." He smiles proud-ly. "We carried on even during the Great Leap. If we couldn't get steel pipe we used iron, and if we couldn't get that we used bam-boo." He picks another bearing, wipes it, inspects it, places it next to the first one.

"One time there wasn't even enough metal for brackets, so I had to carve them from pieces of firewood. One of the old men who had been a carpenter helped me figure out a way to make the brackets interlock with the bamboo, to hold the frame together without nails or screws. Even during the Great Leap our work group had food. Not much maybe. But no-one died." His eyes are shining. A third bearing joins the first two, arranged on the mat in a tiny arc.

He gestures through one of the remaining panes in the front window. "We had a building across the road where everyone lived. Where that computer store is now. The children had lessons in the morning and sorted parts in the afternoon. The older ones began to learn the trade, first assembling the completed parts, later learning millwork or welding. The elderly sat in chairs in front, played *weiqi* or *majiang*. Had tea. Watched the street life. All gone now."

I give him a moment with his thoughts before gently steering him back to why I'm there. "And the museum?" I say.

"Yes, of course. The museum." He wipes and inspects another bearing, frowns, puts it aside. Not with the others. "I did maintenance there, two or three times a week. The plumbing, the oil furnace. Sometimes landscaping, when it was needed. They had some staff, of course, but there was still always work to be done. It was a way I could provide some help to the scholars." "Lihuang—"

He stops, smiles, shakes his head with a chuckle.

"Lihuang had such enthusiasm, but he was also very naive. Crashing about in the open when even a welder knew to keep his head down. I liked him, so I guided him, and after a while we became friends. He knew he could trust me. He told me things when there was no-one else whom he could tell."

I feel a twitch of excitement. I lean further forward.

This is it. This is why I'm in this shop, in this city. Why I've come to China.

I steady my breathing and speak softly but clearly.

"What did he tell you?" I ask.

Ah Xiang takes a deep breath. He looks down at the photo on the table, looks back up at me. Making sure.

He knew he could trust me. But is speaking to me within that trust?

Ah Xiang takes his time. Another bearing rejected, the next two meeting with his approval, the next one again rejected. The arc on the mat grows to a semicircle.

Then he puts down the rag and asks if I'd like more tea. I say yes. He takes the teapot through to the back, out of my sight. I hear water running. So there's a sink back there too.

He has kept Larry's confidence a long time.

Ah Xiang comes back into view in the back room. He crouches over the brick fire pit, gently blows the embers into life and feeds them some fragments of wood from a pile. Smoke drifts up into a waist-high makeshift hood and disappears. There must be a hole cut in the wall. He places a blackened kettle on the grate over the small fire. As he waits for the water to boil he scoops tea leaves from a tin and taps the scoop into the mouth of the teapot. Tap tap tap. When the tea is ready he brings it into the front room on a rectangle of wood, a board-end serving as a tray.

"Lihuang was afraid," he says, setting the tray on the table, "but he was also determined."

No preliminaries. Having decided to trust me he simply carries on from where we left off.

He gets two fresh cups from a shelf on the wall and brings them to the table. "You know that he worked for a radical newspaper?" he asks as he pours, and I nod. He offers my cup to me with both hands. He sits and blows across the surface of his tea. "The people at this newspaper went slightly too far in their support of Deng, and their criticism of the Gang of Four. It wasn't Lihuang's fault. No-one's fault, really. They were young and excited, and incautious. The things they said weren't even particularly dangerous when they said them, but when the wind blew back suddenly they found themselves exposed."

He sips his tea, winces, blows across it again. He sets it to one side and picks another bearing from the bowl. "They shut down the paper and dispersed." He wipes the bearing, examines it, adds it to the growing circle. "Friends of Lihuang found him the job at the museum, translating brochures into English. A safe job. The brochures were carefully inoffensive. The riskiest thing he did during that time was to continue to look for engineering work." He takes the last bearing from the bowl, wipes it, frowns. A discard. The circle on the mat is incomplete by four or five bearings.

I nod again. "Did he ever find any? Engineering work?"

Ah Xiang shakes his head. "I don't know." He gets up and lifts a small tin from a shelf on the wall. "What I do know is a friend of his from the newspaper came to see him at the museum. I don't know his name. I think it was a different friend from the one who got him the job." He opens the tin. It is about half full of bearings of various sizes. He picks out enough to complete the circle.

"This friend, the second one, remembered that Lihuang had been interested in engineering work. He told him about some Third Front projects that were still running, back in the mountains. You know about the Third Front?"

"Yes." I see Judy tracing borders on my skin, marking where Mao's hinterland industrialization would be safe from Western attack.

Ah Xiang lifts a bicycle wheel onto the table. Some of the spokes are pitted with rust and some are missing altogether, but the disassembled hub has been polished to a shine. "This friend had some names," he says. "People who might know people. That wasn't why he had come, though." He runs a rag-covered finger around the circular track inside the hub, and it comes away clean. He fills the track with thick grease from a tube. "He had come to tell Lihuang that one of their old newspaper colleagues had been taken by public security. That they had to assume that he was providing information, and that he knew that Lihuang was working at the museum." He wipes his hands again and sips his tea. "Was it true? I don't know. Maybe. Maybe not. But Lihuang felt he had to leave. So he did. He took another job, somewhere else."

I nod. "At the restaurant, near the mausoleum."

Ah Xiang looks startled. "You already know?"

"Only that he went there, not what happened to him after that. The restaurant is the last place I've been able to trace him to, and it's a dead end. No-one who's there now remembers him."

Ah Xiang wipes his hands and takes a long sip of tea.

"I saw him after that," he says.

The second newspaper friend came back about a month and a half later, this time with something more concrete than names of people who might know people. This time he was in actual contact with a pro-modernization official at a Third Front steel mill who was currently in Beijing quietly looking for engineering professionals. The friend was anxious to introduce Larry to him, but they had to be careful. The climate in Beijing was tense. An anti-Zhou Enlai article at the end of March had sparked a popular pro-Zhou outcry. Crowds of people were laying wreaths to Zhou at the Monument to Martyrs in Tiananmen Square, and in response the Gang of Four had set up a command headquarters in the Great Hall of the People. They would have to keep their heads down.

Larry wasn't worried. He was desperate to meet this engineering contact. In fact, he said that he might actually go down to Tiananmen and lay a wreath for Zhou himself while he was there, which worried his newspaper friend.

Larry told Ah Xiang all of this on the last night they saw each other, over shots of *maotai* in the back of the bike factory. He and the newspaper friend boarded a train to Beijing the next morning, April 3, 1976. He remembers the date because it was his mother's birthday.

"I never heard from Lihuang again after that," Ah Xiang says.

He is still for a moment. Then, one by one, he presses the bearings into the line of grease until they form a complete circle inside the hub.

Wreaths in Tiananmen. Why is that familiar?

We finish our tea, and I thank Ah Xiang for his help. I offer him some American dollars, but he looks a little offended. I've overstepped. I try to fix it by asking more obliquely if there's anything that I might do for him, and he hints that some tea leaves might be welcome. I bow to him from the doorway just before I go.

"Only the eyes," he says again. "Otherwise you are very like him."

He fits the cover over the hub and tightens it with a small wrench.

I walk back toward the hotel. Wreaths in Tiananmen, in April of 1976. There's something there, but it won't come into focus.

I'll have to check my notes.

It's dark by the time I reach the hotel, but I don't go up. I walk past the entrance and down a side street to a brightly lit noodle shop where I have a platter of flat rice noodles with beef and bok choy in thick, dark sauce, and two pots of tea.

I'm stalling. The wreaths in Tiananmen are unsettling. So much so that I'm in no hurry to find out why.

I detour on my way back to the hotel and pick up six cans of Tiger beer and a bag of ice. The musical clock in the hotel lobby starts to play as I come in through the sliding doors. Nine o'clock.

The room's ice bucket holds three of the cans plus enough ice to surround them. While they chill I open a warm one. I get onto the bed, my back propped by pillows, and open my binder against my angled legs.

I start with Larry's letters, but they don't help much. The most recent one, on museum letterhead, is dated February 18, almost two months before the Tiananmen date. It simply says that they may not hear from him for a while, but not to worry. No mention of why, no mention that he's leaving the museum, moving to the restaurant job. Very discreet. It's the last anyone in Canada ever hears from him.

There's nothing in the investigator's reports either, of course.

Why would there be? But I look anyhow. Still stalling. I know where I'll find it.

And I do, on my third beer, in the timeline Judy e-mailed to me as context for Larry's letters.

Zhou Enlai died of cancer in January of 1976. According to Judy, memorial wreaths to Zhou began appearing at the Monument to Martyrs in Tiananmen Square. In late March of 1976, in apparent reaction to an anti-Zhou article in some periodical. Crowds of pro-Zhou demonstrators followed. The Gang of Four responded by denouncing Zhou, and on April 4 security forces cleared away the wreaths after the demonstrators had gone.

The next day, April 5, thousands of demonstrators turned up, followed that evening by thousands of security forces. Some protesters were beaten. Some may have been killed. Reports vary.

I see Judy at a table in a roadhouse, reading over Larry's letters. *At least he wasn't in Beijing on April fifth*, she says. *That's something.*

But he was.

He was leaving for Beijing on April third, on Ah Xiang's mother's birthday. To meet with a contact about a Third Front engineering job. But also—

I squeeze my eyes shut, tightly, and hold the cold can against the middle of my forehead.

But also alive with the idea of placing a wreath to Zhou in Tiananmen Square.

I put my binder and my last beer into my satchel and take the elevator to the roof garden, with wreaths and factories and public security orbiting one another in my head. I snap the binder open and lay out all the pages in a grid on the pavement, held down against the chill night breeze with ornamental rocks. My notes and maps, copies of letters, copies of reports, Judy's e-mail commentary. The big picture.

I sit and stare in the lamplight, sipping beer from a can, hoping to see something different in its totality in the night air than I have found in its specifics in the confines of my room. But I don't.

I now know more than I did, but not what else to do.

What records could there possibly be in Beijing now, especially records that would be available to me? How would I find them? Or read them if I did? The proverbial needle in the proverbial haystack.

But even at that, it's more promising than the scraps that I have about the possible Third Front job. There I don't even know where the haystack is.

Maybe this is it. Maybe I'm done. Further than Uncle Kwok got, but not much. In results, not at all.

I carefully gather the pages into the binder, snap it shut, and open my satchel. And as I shift things to make room, I see a flash of yellow near the bottom. Judy's *I Ching*.

The *I Ching*?

What the fuck.

I use the cover of the binder as a flat surface for the coins, and I toss them until they assemble a hexagram: *Ming I/Darkening of the Light*. I look it up. The judgment is short:

> *Darkening of the light. In adversity*
> *It furthers one to be persevering.*

And though I know this is just random nonsense, I feel encouraged. It will further me to be persevering. That's a nice thing to know. I move to the changing lines. There are two. The oracle for the first begins:

> *Darkening of the light during flight.*
> *He lowers his wings.*
> *The superior man does not eat for three days*
> *On his wanderings,*
> *But he has somewhere to go.*

OK, now that's just silly. I mean, it isn't even *consistent* for Christ's sake. Lowering your wings during flight sounds like taking a break, presumably because of this darkening business, but how do you do that *while* you're on your wanderings? Maybe you have to be the superior man, which I very much doubt I am. And how does it help not to eat for three days? Is it supposed to clear your head or something?

I keep reading. The oracle for the second changing line says:

> *He penetrates the left side of the belly,*
> *One gets at the very heart of the darkening of the light,*
> *And leaves gate and courtyard.*

Yeah, that belly-penetrating thing doesn't sound so good, but this bit at least gets more direct at the end. Leave gate and courtyard.

Hardly a detailed itinerary, but what the hell. It's a next step.

So in the morning I leave gate and courtyard—or at least lobby and sliding doors, which I suppose amounts to the same thing—and step onto the street with my backpack and my satchel and a packet of peanuts from the gift shop.

There's a large tour bus in front of the hotel, and who's there loading it with middle-aged Westerners and Chinese babies but my buddy, the guide from the mausoleum tea house. He spots me right away, and waves. I wave back. After he wrestles the last stroller through the door of the bus behind the last of the parents, I head over to him to say 'hi.'

And then I have a sudden silly impulse.

"What direction are you guys going?" I ask.

He tells them I'm his cousin, that I don't speak English, that I'm coming to help with the bags. I get a fold-down seat near the driver, sitting sideways with my backpack behind my feet.

I didn't pay attention to the name of their actual destination.

It's inland, which is all that matters. The mountains are inland, and the Third Front factories were in the mountains.

Not that I'll find them, of course. That trail is deader than dead. But I'm in China with nothing left but residual momentum, and that momentum points inland. Why not ride it out?

We cruise for hours through flat farmland, watching DVDs in air-conditioned comfort while the people outside tend duck ponds and plough their fields with oxen. The babies keep staring at my eyes.

We stop for lunch at some sort of refuelling station, half-built in the middle of a hard-packed dirt field. The guide shares some rice and an apple with me, and we split my packet of peanuts.

We arrive in a mid-sized city a little after dark. With my back-pack and satchel over my shoulders, I carry two fat suitcases into the hotel lobby, set them down at the check-in counter, and then —with a wink and a nod to the guide—leave through the side door. Two blocks down I cut back to the main street and follow it past a series of cafés and what look like small machine shops until, across a stone bridge, I find another hotel.

This place feels strangely energizing, like maybe I'm not actually done yet. Like maybe there are more tiny pieces here, wherever the hell I am, coiled in wait for me.

But that's probably just the momentum talking. Or the unmediated exhilaration of being completely without a plan for the first time in as long as I can remember. Whatever it is gathers into a knot under my heart that makes me want to double over, but I take deep breaths and smile at the desk staff and they book me into a room.

Ten

I WAKE UP THE NEXT MORNING NOT KNOWING WHERE I AM AT first, and then I chuckle at the realization that that's because I literally don't know where I am. It's exciting. I have a shower and shave and brush my teeth and put on clean clothes and follow the momentum down to the lobby.

Wherever I am, it certainly isn't touristy Nanjing. The warming trays at the breakfast buffet are filled with things I mostly don't recognize, and their labels are only in Chinese. I take some dark noodles and make myself some toast. The only other Westerner in the place is a blond man with blond eyebrows, eating plain congee and shreds of dried tofu, and drinking pale yellow tea. I smile at him as I pass, and he nods.

I spend the morning wandering the neighbourhood. I find a small grocery store and a coin laundry, and some noodle shops that look promising. I may hang out here for a few days. Catch my breath.

I take a late-morning nap in my room and have a late lunch at one of the noodle shops. Then I go back to the hotel, gather my dirty clothes into a plastic grocery bag and haul them to the coin laundry. The blond man with the blond eyebrows is there, folding a dryer-load of pastel no-iron shirts. We nod to each other. I open a washer and dump my clothes in, and then realize that I've forgotten laundry soap. Damn.

I look around. There's a coin-operated machine on the back wall with pictures of tiny boxes of detergent across the top. But when I get to it I see that a scrap of paper with some Chinese characters scrawled on it has been taped over its coin mechanism. Presumably the Chinese for *Out of Order*.

"Son of a *bitch*," I say, and slap the machine with the palm of my hand.

"Ah, you speak English, thank God," the blond man says. "I was afraid I would have to make do with hand gestures." He holds out a small box of detergent, like the ones pictured on the dispenser. It's about a third full. "I had the same problem earlier in the week, so today I brought my own. From the grocery store." He gestures vaguely toward the door, with the box. "I am done for now. You are welcome to what is left."

He has a slight accent, hard to place. Europe, but beyond that I can't quite tell.

I take the box. "Thank you. You're very kind. If I'm in town long enough I'll return the favour."

He holds out his right hand. "Silvio Mondschein. My pleasure."

I shake his hand. "Jason Lavoie."

"La-voy?" he says. "But surely this is a French name, La-*vwah*, yes?"

"We pronounce it differently in our family."

"Hmm. The accent is not English, so perhaps on your father's side you are American? From, say, Louisiana? I say your father, of course, because you do not have an Asian surname. Or perhaps *Franco-canadien*?" He raises a blond eyebrow.

"Yeah. That last one." He's starting to creep me out a little. But he gave me soap.

He bows his head modestly. "Thank you Jason La-*vwah*, for that is what I shall call you. You will not budge me on this. I honour your heritage."

Over the next few days I end up spending a fair amount of time with Silvio Mondschein, mostly because he's the only other person at the hotel who speaks English, though he never quite stops creeping me out. We fall into a routine of having dinner together at the buffet.

"You are a musician?" he says one evening as we're leaving the dining room, spreading his hands as if to hug me, though he doesn't. "How excellent. And a composer? Even better. Do you have any of your music with you?"

"Well, no. But I have a few pieces posted on my web site."

"I should like to hear some. Will you oblige me with the address of your site?" From the breast pocket of his blazer he produces a maroon notebook with gold-edged ivory pages. The spine crackles with newness as he opens it to the first page. It's blank. He uncaps a dark malachite fountain pen and hands it to me. I print the URL carefully along the top line. The ink is a rich royal blue.

"I am obliged," he says as he slips the notebook back into his blazer. "I believe the hotel business centre has internet access, though it is probably censored. I assume the authorities will have no reason to be concerned about your site?"

The opera isn't far enough along for me to have posted anything about it, especially not a plot outline. "No reason."

"Excellent. When we meet next I may have comments. My thanks again."

And he turns and strides briskly to the main entrance, to the revolving door. The light of the setting sun glints off of the panels as they spin. I shade my eyes. "Start with *Infernal Variations*," I call out, as Silvio Mondschein revolves through into the cool of the evening.

He's as good as his word. As I'm eating my toast the next morning Silvio Mondschein brings his tea over to my table.

"This is a marvellous thing, Jason La-*vwah*, that you write this music! I am a little impressed. Not overwhelmed, I am sorry"—he pouts for a moment—"but still, it is good, solid, *Canadian* music." He sits across from me and opens his notebook. Two or three pages are now filled with tidy handwriting.

I finish chewing, and swallow. "Canadian music has a style?" I finally say.

He shakes his head. "No, not Canadian music. But the Canadian *character*, yes, of course. Your music is like your nation"—he puts on a hearty voice and moves his bent arms rhythmically, as if marching—"polite and dependable"—he chuckles, lowers his arms, goes back to his normal voice—"with a little bit of the mandatory diversity and not, I think, very much of the adventurous."

His smile has a little bit of the smugness and not, I think, very much of the apologetic.

"I see." And I give him my best *who the fuck do you think you are* look. How do you respond to shit like this? "Don't you think that's just a little oversimplified?"

He tilts his head and pouts again. "Oh, I have bruised your artistic feelings. My profound apologies, Jason La-*vwah*. I have overstepped. Or is it your patriotism I have bruised?"

I flip the rest of my piece of toast onto my plate, knocking the plastic jam packet onto the table. "It's just a pretty glib dismissal of my life's work so far, that's all. Forgive me for being a little touchy about it."

"No no, this is not my intention. I am truly sorry. I do not mean to be dismissive. These are simply observations on your style."

"Dismissive observations."

"I am sorry you see them that way. I have expressed myself badly. And yet I stand by what I have said."

I nod. "You want to suck and blow."

This stops him dead. The expression baffles him. He wrestles with it for a moment, his face grave.

"If this is some erotic invitation—"

"No, no." I laugh. "It's an idiom. It means, like ... like you want to be able to do two inconsistent things at the same time."

His face relaxes. "Ah, OK. This is a strange idiom. 'Suck and blow?'"

"It's actually 'suck and blow at the same time'. You got the short version."

"Ah. This makes somewhat more sense. And the two inconsistent things in this case?"

"You want to stand by your insult without being insulting."

He holds both hands up, palms toward me, and waves them back and forth. "No no, this is not meant to be an insult. I think it must be my English."

I think it must be your pretentiousness, I think. But I don't say it. I'm Canadian.

"Let me try to explain," he goes on, flattening his notebook on the table. "Your *Infernal Variations*, for example."

"Yes?" I say warily.

"It is my comment about the lack of adventurousness that offends you, yes? But this is simply a fact. Your—"

"So far you aren't making it any better."

He sniffs. "Perhaps you will give me the opportunity?"

"All right, sorry. Go on."

"Thank you. Your theme. It is a pleasant tune, but for the most part conventionally tonal. There is nothing wrong with this. Much can be done with such a tune, especially in a set of variations. What you do with it is pleasant, certainly, and it has an energy."

"But?"

"Well for one thing, harmonically there is little in it that one could not find in, say, Debussy. But more important, it is so relentlessly *linear*. Variation one: linear. Variation two: linear. Variation three: linear. And so to the end."

"But that's the nature of the form. The theme has a line, and the variations pick it up."

"Yes, they can, to be sure. But do they *have* to? Again, this is not meant to be an insult. It is merely an observation about style." He rests his elbow on the table and draws his fingers along his jawline, his eyes lowered. Then he looks up, earnest. "Let me put it this way. Perhaps it will be clearer and less fraught." He moves his hand into the space between us, palm down, fingers spread toward me. "You are the classicist—this is a word? Classicist?—rather than the romantic."

This stops me.

"That's it?" I say. "That's all you're saying? Because it sure didn't sound like it."

He raises his palm toward me and waves his spread fingers. "No, I know it did not. This is my fault, of course. Again, I apologize."

"Classical versus romantic? That's your point?"

"To simplify it a little, yes. Or perhaps even better, the Apollonian and the Dionysian. Your style is more the Apollonian. Orderly, linear." He smiles wryly. "Like your country."

"And you think I should be more Dionysian? Wilder, more chaotic?"

He shakes his head vigorously. "No no no, not should, not *should*. Again I am misunderstood. I am not giving advice. This is entirely *your* artistic choice."

There is a quiet pause. He lifts his cup, sips his tea. Peers at me over the rim.

"But of course it would give your work more balance," he says.

This city seems to be primarily industrial. It occupies both sides of a broad river valley and the top of a ridge to one side. The hotel is in the lower town, nestled in the crook of the ridge, well back from the rail yard and the riverside docks but not up with the lavish gardens and public buildings along the ridge's brow.

There is a tidy cliff-top park beside what appears to be some sort of municipal building, with pruned trees and sturdy wooden benches and a spectacular view of the lower town and the river beyond. I take to sitting there for hours at a time, eating unfamiliar salty packaged snacks from the hotel shop, drawing crude landscape sketches on the blank sides of the photocopies in my binder, and generally just wondering *what the fuck do I do now?*

"But you must not give up! This would be tragic."

I've made the mistake of telling Silvio Mondschein how I came to be here. The essentials, anyhow: Larry, the letters, Ah Xiang in his bicycle shop. The cold trail growing colder.

"What else can I do?" I gesture to the open binder on the dining table. "I have pieces, fragments of pieces even, and they're fine as far as they go, but the point is that they don't go anywhere."

"Go in what sense?"

"Are you serious? Go in the sense of get me anywhere."

"Step by step."

"Yes. How else?"

Silvio Mondschein leans toward me across the table. "But Jason La-*vwah*, we have already *had* this conversation." I look at him blankly, and he shakes his head.

"All right," he says, "let me try it this way." He lifts his hands in front of him as if holding a small ball. "How one structures the world depends on who one *is*. To the particle physicist, the essence of the universe is particles. This is self-evident. To the mathematician it is, let us say, algorithms. To the MBA it is commodities. To the lawyer it is liability. This is why they drink. Each has its obvious limitations."

"So?"

He crosses his arms on the tabletop and leans closer. Like he's sharing a confidence. "To you, my musical friend, it is *line*. Occurrences in time, one leading to the next. Patterns, sequences. Occasional interruptions, but never for long. This is *your* limitation." He sits back and places his palms on the binder, fingers spread. "The limitation is not in these pages. It is in you, in your imagination. To move on this quest you must move away from your Apollo. You must embrace your Dionysos."

"So now you *are* giving me advice?"

He sits back against his chair and smiles. "Yes. I suppose now I am."

Silvio Mondschein is so full of shit.

For the next couple of days I avoid him. He was amusing at first, and it's been nice to have someone to speak English with, but he's starting to piss me off. That backpedaling after he insulted my music. This bullshit about how I should keep on looking. Dionysos my ass. I'm done. There's nowhere left to look and that isn't going to change, no matter how much Eurotrash pseudo-intellectualism you fling at it.

I connect to my web site from the hotel business centre and muck about for an afternoon, clearing out stale posts and reconfiguring a couple of links to make the site more intuitive. I sit in the ridge-top park with a paper cup of strong tea and a pad of manuscript paper and I work and rework some ideas for the opera, but nothing quite comes together. I'm not sure what the problem is. It just all seems a little too—

A little too—

God help me, I will *not* say *linear.*

What I do not do is call home.

What would I say?

What I do not do is make plans.

Moment to moment.

Occurrences in time, leading nowhere.

Silvio Mondschein comes upon me at dusk in a tea shop near the hotel. I'm at a window table, sipping oversteeped oolong and reading my gift-shop *Journey to the West* abridgment. He is passing on the sidewalk. He pauses and bends to identify the book, and when I look up at him through the window his face and my reflection momentarily align, his blonde eyebrows above my false eyes. Then he moves, and the moment is gone.

He comes in and joins me, of course.

The server brings another cup and pours more water into the pot from a blackened steel kettle. Silvio Mondschein fills each of our cups, raises his in a brief eye-level salute, and takes a sip. If it's bitter to him he doesn't let on.

"Monkey King," he says, gesturing toward my book.

"Yeah. And his companion Pigsy." I turn the book to the blurb on the back cover. "Apparently I will be charmed by their mythic adventures battling demons and Taoists as they guide the Tang monk Xuanzong to India to obtain authentic scriptures from the Buddha."

Silvio Mondschein swirls his tea in his cup and lifts it to his nose, his eyes closed, savouring the aroma. "You should be careful what you read."

I fold the corner of a page to mark my place. "Why?"

He sets his cup down. "Stories shape us more than we realize. When I read Robertson Davies, for example, I am drawn to the rich perversities of academia, which I otherwise find terribly dull. When I read John Updike I feel vaguely dissatisfied with my marriage. When I read Ian Fleming I wish to have a cruel mouth and drink vodka martinis."

I look up from putting by book into my bag. "I didn't know you were married." He doesn't wear a ring.

"I am not." He smiles. "This is my point exactly."

Sleeve has tried to explain derivatives to me but I've never managed to grasp them. Apparently they have no intrinsic value of their own. Their value somehow comes from the value of whatever less abstract thing they're derived from.

"So why not just buy *that* then?" I always ask.

And Sleeve always rolls his eyes.

I feel like a derivative. A derivative with a binder full of useless photocopies. A derivative with nowhere to go.

And I set down my bottle and laugh at myself and pick it up again.

One morning I take my tea and my satchel to a small pavilion in the ridge-top garden with a view down the river into the misty distance. I flip to the back of my binder, to the roof-garden *I Ching* reading that prompted me out of Nanjing how long ago? A week? Ten days? But there's nothing there any more. No call to perseverance, no cheeky riding of the momentum like a wave. Nothing to lead me anywhere past this city, past this day. Past the next mouthful of tea.

What the hell, I think. *Different day.* I take the scuffed yellow book and the coins out of my satchel and cast my fortune again. This time I get *Kuai, Break-through.* I quickly read the judgment, then carefully write it out on a clean sheet of foolscap.

> *Break-through. One must resolutely make the matter known*
> *At the court of the King.*
> *It must be announced truthfully. Danger.*
> *It is necessary to notify one's own city.*
> *It does not further to resort to arms.*
> *It furthers one to undertake something.*

Break-through sounds good. I could use a little breakthrough.

Not so keen on danger.

Otherwise it doesn't do much for me. Make *what* known, at the court of *which* King? And if my own city refers to Calgary, I still can't bring myself to call anyone there.

Not resorting to arms should be easy enough.

I straighten my own arms behind myself, clasp my hands together and lean backward. My spine crackles between my shoulder blades. It feels nice. I lean my head to the right, and then to the left, stretching out my neck muscles. They're really tight. I massage them with my fingertips.

So say we read this broadly, in context. Take the court of the King to mean the seat of the government. That would be Beijing. Does that mean that I made the wrong call when I left Nanjing? Should I be following the Beijing dead end, rather than vacillating here on this sham path to the Third Front dead end?

Undertake something. No shit. But undertake what?

Maybe there's more in the changing line. I write it on the foolscap too, under the judgment.

> *There is no skin on his thighs,*
> *And walking comes hard.*
> *If a man were to let himself be led like a sheep,*
> *Remorse would disappear.*

I could certainly do with less remorse.

Walking comes hard. I need to be led. Led by whom? I don't know anyone here, or at least no-one other than Silvio Mondschein, and at this point I wouldn't trust that pompous pricklet to lead me to the fucking buffet. Led by the oracle? Or is that just circular?

I open the binder and take out the foolscap page. I hold it at eye level, try to take it all in at once.

Breakthrough.

Beijing would be going back, not breaking through.

I suppose the Third Front projects *could* be considered the court, if the King means Mao. The court of last resort?

Fuck this nonsense. What was I thinking?

I stuff the page into my pocket and start back down the ridge.

With fewer clothes I have to wash them more often. I can't seem to find the detergent Silvio Mondschein gave me, so I get some of my own.

Everything is starting to fade. Shirts, pants. Underwear. The only thing not fading, or at least not noticeably, is Miranda's phone number inside the waistband of my jeans.

That is one tough-assed laundry marker.

The translucent light panels behind shelves of bar stock make the bottles glow, their labels dark silhouettes against amber whiskies, sapphire liqueurs, diamond-sharp vodkas and gins. Silvio Mondschein flattens my crumpled note against the polished mahogany surface and peers at it through tiny rimless glasses.

Yeah, I know. But at least it's the bar rather than the damn buffet.

"But this is perfectly clear to me," he says. "As I have said to you, it is your linear Apollonian thinking that you must break through."

I pick a cashew from a bowl of nuts on the bar. "Yeah, right. I should move forward on what is fundamentally a linear journey by some sort of lateral means."

"Yes. Precisely."

"But that makes no sense. I'm looking for an actual person. I'm following the evidence. It's a linear process. Step by step."

"But there is no next linear step. You have exhausted your evidence."

He has a point.

Or does he?

"No, it's no good to just take off in some random direction. If the trail here is cold then I just have to rethink it, figure out where to pick it up again."

Silvio Mondschein gives me an *oh you poor little country mouse* smile and slowly shakes his head. "Not random. You miss my point." He taps his temple with his forefinger. "The mind is a large place. It has regions that we do not get to with reason alone. This is why we have myth, and ritual, and art, and"—he taps the note-book page on the bar—"this *Book of Change* that you find so intriguing."

He picks up the page from the bar and holds it curled length-wise between his thumb and fingers so that it projects out at me like a blade. "That your so linear mind is so taken with this glorious old gibberish is perhaps the most interesting thing about you, Jason La-*vwah*." He pulls my shirt pocket open with his other hand and tamps the page down into it with two fingers. He pats the pocket flat and leaves his palm there against my chest. "Trust the part of your mind that speaks to you through this nonsense. Not random, no. But also not linear."

And then he's gone.

He's full of shit, of course. He makes it sound nice, in his clever clever little Silvio Mondschein way, but he's basically telling me that to follow a rational path I have to make irrational choices.

Fuck him.

I sit up until almost dawn making pot after pot of tea, re-reading my notes and Larry's letters, re-thinking how I've managed to get as far as I have, re-considering how it might all lead rationally to the next step. And as my eyes sag, and my pages and Larry's blur togeth-er, the bitter, oversteeped realization can no longer be avoided.

The next step is the Third Front factory where Larry may once have worked.

And I have no rational way of finding it.

God damn that blond-headed son-of-a-bitch.

I need to lighten up. I leave my backpack in the luggage room of the hotel, keeping only keys and wallet in my pockets and passport, notebook, *I Ching* and binder of letters in my army surplus satchel.

It furthers one to undertake something? OK, fine. And if walk-ing comes skin-off-the-thighs hard, then I guess I'd better ride.

On a semi-educated guess as to where the Third Front factories might have been I take a cab as far out of town as the driver is prepared to go, and when he drops me there I stick out my thumb.

It takes me an hour to realize that the thumb doesn't mean anything here. It takes me another twenty minutes to wave down my first truck. It takes me three tries to figure out that no-one hitches for free, and two rides to realize the importance of agreeing on a price in advance. I don't know if it's furthering me, but I'm damn sure undertaking something.

I keep moving inland, changing rides whenever a driver veers too far from my presumed course. From a bench in the back of a pickup I watch fishermen pole flat boats along a steel grey river. From the cab of a diesel panel truck I see flooded rice fields shine like window glass in the late afternoon sun, the driver's hand weaving intricate patterns with the knob of an arm-long gearshift as he grinds us along a narrow ridge to the next valley, and the next. Coming on to evening I find myself in a town too small to have street lights but big enough to have a couple of guest houses, and I decide that I've undertaken enough for one day.

Wherever I am, the language has changed. I can barely make myself understood to the squat woman in the doorway of the second guest house, but with my schoolbook Mandarin supplemented with nods, smiles and hand gestures, we settle on a comparative pittance for a night's accommodation. The room is just that —four walls and a curtained door, with a low, too-short sleeping pallet and a narrow unglazed window looking onto a fenced chicken yard. The evening meal—rice with a few strips of unseasoned meat and a few leaves of some sort of vegetable—is tasty, and apparently included.

After dinner I follow the noise down the main street to what I later decide to call The Pub: an open-front concrete-block building at the town crossroads with mismatched tables and a long unvarnished counter behind which a man in a frayed Cinzano apron is serving what looks like rice liquor from an unlabelled jug.

Three of the four tables are crowded with men in canvas trousers and T-shirts smoking hand-rolled cigarettes and playing *majiang*. At the fourth table, sipping a pale yellow liquid from a short tumbler and reading the *International Herald Tribune*, is Silvio Mondschein.

"Non-rational," he says as I sit down across from him. "Not irrational. There is a distinction."

And somehow I'm not even surprised to see him.

I sleep late the next morning. When I rise there's no-one there and no sign of breakfast, so I wander down to the crossroads to The Pub, where I manage to get some congee and tea.

After I've eaten I approach a small group of local men at a table near the back. We manage to communicate in fragments of Mandarin and scraps of English. How they happen to know any English is too subtle a notion for me to unearth in the circumstances.

They pass around my uncle's picture, study it earnestly, mumble to one another in a dialect I can't make out. The one nearest me passes it back with nicotine-stained fingers and says that maybe this man was here, maybe a long time ago, maybe not him. Someone in the village to the east may know more. I ask which way is east, and they point behind me.

I join Silvio Mondschein at the table near the street. He has a pot of tea and two cups.

"They are laughing, you know," he says. "No, don't look, they are not going to be obvious about it. They have no idea who your uncle is or where he could be. They're chuckling inside about the Chinese with funny eyes who can't speak the language, who believes whatever he is told."

I shrug. "Maybe," I say. I'm almost past caring anyhow.

Silvio Mondschein pours us both tea and we sip it in silence, the only sounds the stirrings of distant birds and the *majiang* players at the back table.

"Your uncle doesn't even exist," Silvio Mondschein says after a while, setting his cup down on the table. "You made him up."

"But here's his picture," I say. Producing it from my shirt pocket, dog-eared and cracked by now, but undeniably tangible. "See?"

"Hmm. Fair enough. Then maybe he made you up."

"Maybe we made *you* up."

A solemn nod. "Yes. This is much more likely."

My mother played the piano with one hand.

My viola trio derived its value from Dante.

The next day, or perhaps the day after, the same group of men is at the back of The Pub, playing the same game. Near them this time is a table of three or four Americans, already shitfaced on the harsh local liquor, barely past noon. They arrived last night in an olive green Range Rover and essentially took over the guest house. They ask, in English, about some tombs that are supposed to be near here. The *majiang* players pretend not to understand a word. The Americans ask again, louder, with hand gestures, like they're dealing with idiots. Idiots who haven't learned the rules, who have somehow let their country slip a little too far off the Pennsylvania norm for the travellers' convenience.

"I don't get that," I say to Silvio Mondschein, gesturing toward them with my head.

"Get what?"

"That. Those Americans."

Silvio Mondschein turns toward the back of the room, turns back. "What about them?"

I shrug. "Just them. Their attitude. The lack of respect. I don't get it."

Silvio Mondschein smiles. "That is because you are not a tourist. You are a pilgrim."

Another day. I spread what little I have of Uncle Larry on the scarred tabletop like a tarot layout. A picture. Six photocopied letters. The map with my markings. The little notebook with my *I Ching* castings, now up to about a dozen, none of them very helpful. It doesn't amount to much. I flatten my palms on the pages, line up their corners. I shake my head. "I don't know which way to go any more," I say.

Silvio Mondschein nods gravely at the little tableau, then looks up. "Which way makes you feel most apprehensive?"

I look out through the open front of The Pub at to the crossroads, turning my attention to each of the four streets in turn, gauging with my gut. "That way," I say, pointing toward the setting sun, down a gravel road into the hills.

"Go there," Silvio Mondschein says.

Eleven

AFTER CONSIDERABLE AWKWARD HAGGLING WITH ONE OF THE back-table men, I exchange my wristwatch and much of my remaining cash for a basic one-speed bicycle. Its chrome handlebars are pitted with decades of rust and its tires are patched and worn almost smooth, but it's well-maintained and functional. I think of Ah Xiang and his resilient work group. I imagine the frame of my new bicycle made of carved hardwood blocks and interlocking bamboo.

I pedal out of the village before the dawn mist has fully cleared, weaving unsteadily on the packed dirt road until I get the feel of the bike's handling. Around mid-morning I reach the edge of a river valley with a crude switchback path down to the water. The bouncing of the bike as I descend rattles my spine and my teeth, and when I nearly lose the track at the fourth or fifth turn I give up and walk the bike the rest of the way down.

My village landlady has packed me a generous serving of rice and vegetables wrapped in brown paper. I eat half of it on the riverbank with my fingers and wash it down with handfuls of cool water.

The path along the river is so rutted it makes the bike all but useless, but I persevere. I'm going to feel it in the morning, though.

Near nightfall I turn left, away from the river and follow the glow of distant light down a gravel road to a hamlet of a few one-room huts, where I exchange the rest of my cash for a simple meal and a night on a dirt floor under—strangely—an antique Hudson's Bay blanket.

I sleep uneasily. My muscles ache, and my head feels strange.

I leave the hamlet the next morning on foot, continuing away from the river on the gravel road. A thin morning soup has settled my stomach somewhat, but my head is still foggy. I leave the bike with my host family in exchange for some salt fish and a bag of root vegetables I don't recognize.

By mid-morning the gravel has given way to dirt. It's smooth, so I take off my shoes. After a while I don't seem to have them any more. I must've pitched them somewhere. I'm not sure why I would, but there you go. It doesn't really matter. The path is smooth.

It leads to a rough track along a small river. I stop and drink from cupped hands. I try to peel one of the root vegetables with my pocket knife but it slips and slices my thumb so I throw it into the river. There's blood on the vegetable now so I throw it in too. I carry on walking, sucking on my thumb until the bleeding stops.

I chew salt fish until I'm thirsty, then stop for more water, then chew some more, and soon I have no more fish, though I still have water. I can't find my root vegetables. I must have forgotten to pick them back up after one of my water-stops.

I march along the dusty river-track for what feels like several hours, yet the sun barely moves in the sky. Where am I going?

The answer has burned down to basics.

That way. I'm going that way.

I walk.

I sleep under a hedge.

I sleep in a half-collapsed hut.

I sleep under a rock overhang that almost keeps the rain off.

That way.

Late one morning I come upon a rough plank bridge over the small river. As long as it's here, I may as well cross. My satchel snags on the makeshift railing, which stops me. Why do I need a satchel? I open it in the middle of the bridge and sort through its contents. A map. A notebook. A binder with some copies of some letters. What good are these things? They probably have some use, but I can't think what it is. I put them aside. Maybe it'll come to me.

More things. A passport. Mine. A photograph. My uncle. Uncle Larry.

I should find Uncle Larry.

I try to stick Uncle Larry's picture into my passport on top of mine but all I have to stick it with is spit and it won't stay. I try three times, then drop them both off the bridge and watch them drift away around a bend. I like the way they turn in the current as they go, so I drop the map too, and then the notebook. I drop the pages from the binder one at a time, waiting until each disappears around the bend before dropping the next one. Then I drop the binder. Then I drop the satchel. The satchel catches on the bottom at first, but soon the current wiggles it free and it follows everything else out of sight. I wave to it as it goes.

That was nice.

My pockets are uncomfortably full, so I empty them. As long as I'm here. As long as I'm letting things go. Wallet. Keys. Three funny coins with square holes in them. Nothing I need. They all go into the river.

I try skipping the coins across the surface, but there's too much current.

I keep one thing. A yellow book. It's a nice yellow.

I carry on across the bridge. There's a path on the other side, so I follow it.

There are thin grey clouds on the horizon, but overhead the sky is wide open and the sun is making my head uncomfortably hot. I

could use a hat. Maybe my shirt could be a hat. I take it off and try
to wrap it around my head like a turban, but I don't know how to
wrap a turban so it doesn't work too well. I try tying the sleeves
around my forehead, which helps the back of my neck but not the
top of my head, and the sleeve-ends block my vision, so after while
I just give up and toss the shirt into the bushes.

My legs are too warm, too, in my blue jeans. This isn't weather
for blue jeans. Too hot. I should turn them into cut-offs. I'm about
to take them off to make cut-offs when I realize I've lost my knife,
so I leave them on and keep walking. I can't shake the cut-off idea,
though. If I could turn my jeans into cut-offs, maybe I could use the
discarded leg-pieces to make some kind of hat. A win-win idea. But
I don't have a knife. I just have to be a bit resourceful. What did
people do to make cut-offs before there were knives? Besides use
scissors, of course. Which I also don't have.

I have an idea.

I wade into the river to where the rocks are, pick out three or
four about the size of baking potatoes, take them to the shore, and
smash them together until one of them breaks at a sharp enough
angle to use as a makeshift blade. It takes a long time. Then it takes
even longer to make a hole in the denim and to work the stone-blade
around the leg. It isn't actually all that sharp. I could really use a
knife. I wonder what happened to my knife? Or scissors. Scissors
would also work.

Eventually I manage to cut away both legs. They're a little uneven, and very ragged, but they fit nicely. I try to pull one of the
discarded leg-pieces onto my head like a toque, but it's too small.
So is the other one. So I fold them and leave them under a tree, and
get back on the trail.

Late in the day the river winds through a small village: a dozen or
so low brick buildings, a goose pond, some animal pens. A few men
are coming in from the fields. Ahead of me on the riverbank two

women are scooping river water into metal pots, maybe to prepare the evening meal. They stop chatting and look up at me as I pass, but I don't stop, don't speak. This isn't the kind of place where Uncle Larry would be. I don't have his picture any more anyhow.

And the local dialect sounds funny. I don't like it.

I keep walking.

Not far past the edge of the village the trees and bushes grow thin and soon stop altogether, the river now only a muddy trickle, but I can still make out the path across the scrubland. The ground here is rocky and hard, and I have to watch my step. I smell something faint but rich. Manure, I think I look up the bank, away from the river, and spot what looks like a large vegetable field a kilometre or so away, apparently doing well. Not like here by the river. Here there are just clumps of brown grass and bony-looking bushes cowering against the dusty ground. Not even good grazing land. Strange that things are worse here by the river.

I wonder if there are channels, diverting the water from the river to land more suited to growing things like vegetables. I wonder who dug them, and how long ago, but I keep walking, and soon the vegetable fields and their manure smell drop away behind me.

Near a bend in the river is a rock outcropping as big as a bungalow, which I pick my way carefully around. When I clear it and can look ahead again I see something amazing. A hundred paces or so farther along, in the midst of an otherwise barren stretch of land, there is a tree, a marvellous tree, leaning out over the meagre stream. A pine of some sort, I think. Very old, I think. Its bark is grey and deeply furrowed. Its barrel-thick trunk rises barely a hand's breadth from its exposed roots before it kinks sharply inland, spirals up to the height of my shoulders, and bursts into a melee of misshapen branches that twist back toward the water as if blown there by a powerful, silent wind. From the tops of the branches thick clumps of long green needles stretch up and away from the dusty ground.

This is a good place to stop.

I'd like to eat, but I have no food.

I should probably have stopped at the vegetable field. But that would've been stealing. Sleeve wouldn't have approved.

I'd like a drink, but the river here is too muddy and thin.

Didn't I have a container once, that I could have used to carry water with me?

I don't remember any more. I'm tired, and sweaty from walking.

I will rest.

I carefully place my yellow book at the base of the tree. It will be my pillow. When I am satisfied with how I've placed it, I turn around and settle myself onto the ground, adjusting position until my head lines up with the yellow book. I fold my hands carefully across my naked chest.

This is a good place to rest.

A breeze drifts across from the small river, drying the sweat on my ribs and making me shiver. It has an edge. I wonder if the weather is turning. I wonder if discarding my shirt was such a good idea after all. The green needles overhead rustle together in the breeze, battlefield comrades whispering as they wait for dawn. Legions of slim green lances, angling up and away from me to defend me from the sky.

I continue walking until I reach a downward-sloping hill of rocks and rubble. It hurts to climb down it, but that's the direction I'm going so I kind of have to. At the foot of the rubble hill the land levels out again. In the distance a band of crimson stretches to either side as far as I can see, and just beyond it a range of low, golden-brown hills is beginning to darken as the sun settles behind them. *There*, I think, looking at the lavender shadows between the hills. *I should go there.*

I keep walking.

A kilometre or so along I notice a tangy, humid smell, and the ground begins to soften. The crimson band turns out to be a swath of grassy plants in a boggy, slow-moving river. In the creeping twilight their reflection makes the water itself look red. A light mist drifts among them along the surface, broken every few metres by yellowish boulders of varying sizes. The water can't be all that deep. I'll just wade through it.

The boggy ground feels strangely warm as I approach the edge. I take a cautious first step into the water and recoil with a yelp. It's blistering hot. The mist along the surface is *steam*.

I back away and consider. The daylight is fading, and there's no shelter on this side of the wetland. I look upstream, then down. There must be a bridge or something somewhere, though I can't see one from here.

Pick a direction.

Left. Upstream.

I walk for about twenty minutes without finding a bridge, or a ferry, or even anything resembling a ford. I turn around and walk back the other way for what must be close to an hour, with no better luck. There's no way across other than wading. I test the water to see if it's any cooler this far downstream, but it's still scalding. The hot spring that feeds it must be *damn* hot.

The daylight is down to a narrow band of washed-out blue along the horizon and I'm no further ahead, but I'm determined to make it to the hills before nightfall. I walk slowly along the bank, peering into the near-darkness for the tightest grouping of boulders I can find.

There, that looks promising. Five metres or so to the first one, a step or two at most between each of the rest, and then about a ten metre sprint to the far shore. How hard can it be?

I head into the river at a run, partly to make use of the momentum but mostly to commit myself before I can change my mind. The pain is sudden and intense, as though the red water is actually boiling. With each step I lift my foot as high as I can above the surface, maximizing its time in the cooling air before it plunges back in. By the time I reach the first boulder both legs are pink and puffy to mid-calf, and even on the cool rock it hurts to stand. Thankfully this boulder is big enough to sit on. There won't be room on any of the rest.

I wait as long as I can, blowing gently along the surface of my skin to cool it. It doesn't seem to help much. I have to keep going before I lose sight of the rocks in the dark. The next one is only two steps away, one with each tender foot, but since it's only about the size of a pizza box I have to stand when I get there, dancing from one foot to the other to give each a small respite. The single steps to each of the next two rocks spare one foot at a time, and the one after that is reachable with a short leap without touching the water at all. As I dance there from foot to foot I'm caught between my delight at having made it this far and my certainty that I can't manage the final dash to the far shore.

Ten metres. Ten or twelve steps at best, probably more. At least five steps with each foot. But then I'm there. Then I can rest, and recover.

Once more I fling myself in quickly, yelping audibly as each foot comes down. Eight steps, nine steps, ten steps, goddamn *eleven* steps, the last one puddle-shallow and then I'm out, crashing down onto the warm boggy shore, crying up at the darkened sky. The muscles of my feet are loose on the bone like overcooked chicken. What was I *thinking* when I pitched my shoes?

There's no possibility of finding shelter. I can't move, except maybe on my hands and knees, and I can't see anything other than the final wisp of daylight slipping away behind the hills. I might as well try to sleep.

But I can't. I can't touch my feet to the ground without screaming, let alone put their own whole weight on them, even lying down. After trying for a while I end up crawling to a nearby tree and propping my legs across its root so that my feet dangle in the air. It's an odd position for sleeping, but the breeze against them is soothing and I eventually doze off.

And before I know it it's morning. It's cool, and heavily overcast, and my feet somehow seem to be fine. Skin normal colour, flesh firm and tight to the bone I touch each one gently with my fingertip. No pain. I stand up. Never better. I trot in place in amazement. I feel like I could walk for kilometres. It doesn't make any sense, but there it is.

So I go on.

I must have gotten disoriented during the night, though, because there are no hills on this side of the river. The ground here is flat, and thickly wooded with white birch and tall pines. I'm pretty sure that's the right direction, though, so I guess I'll have to go through.

There doesn't seem to be an actual path, but there's very little underbrush and the forest floor is quite even, so the going is pretty smooth, even with bare feet. The biggest problem will be staying oriented. With the cloud cover there isn't much sun to begin with, and what little there is won't likely make it far into the depths of the wood.

I make my way in cautiously.

The forest is delightful at first: There's a comfortably springy layer of pine needles underfoot, and the bright autumn-yellow birch leaves make the thin cloudlight seem almost cheerful. After a while, though, I lose sight of the way I came in, and as the light thins the forest seems to draw in closer with each step. Soon I'm stubbing my toes against hidden roots, and unseen branches are drawing sharp, sticky needles across my unprotected cheeks.

And then I hear sounds from above. Heavy, crashing sounds, like falling branches; like too-large birds landing on too-small trees.

Do they have eagles in China?

I should ask Judy if I see her.

There is a crash off to the left. I turn quickly toward it and I think I see movement, but I can't be sure in the dim light. Then there's another crash back behind me, and what sounds like heavy wing-beats. Then another crash right overhead, and a rasping bird-call that sounds like ... that *almost* sounds like *Jason-n-n*. But it isn't, of course.

This forest is clearly creeping me out. I'm getting out of here. I start to run.

Branches slap my face as I duck and weave through the trees. I'm trying to figure out if I see a patch of light up ahead when I nearly take a jagged twig in the eye, spotting it at the last instant and instinctively lurching sideways but still getting a nasty scratch along my temple to the top of my ear. The crashing is louder and more frequent now, and all around me, the bird-cries still sounding uncannily like my name. *Jason-n-n-n. Jason-n-n-n.*

The cries never sound like *Lavoie-e-e-e*, though, which helps me keep my perspective.

Not that the birds would get the pronunciation right.

It *is* a patch of light, and growing lighter. It's the edge of the forest. The trees are thinner here, so I put on an extra burst of speed. There's a particularly loud crash just behind me and to my left as I come flying out past the last of the pines and onto what seems like a moonscape. Flakes of something corrosive are falling from the overcast sky, and black sand scorches the soles of my feet.

Out of the damn frying pan.

I dash across the black desert toward what looks like it might be a stream, dodging the scorching flakes as best I can. And it is a stream, thank Christ, and although tepid and sluggish it's a *serious* improvement over the burning black sand. Or the boiling red river, for that matter. I sluice myself with it to wash off the flakes, and follow it until they stop falling.

The stream ends in a waterfall, dropping maybe thirty metres, creating a mist that obscures the uneven land below. A little way beyond there seems to be a gorge, cutting across my path, and then beyond that another, and another. The mist keeps shifting. To the right I think I see a bridge. Another one beyond it, maybe. Hard to tell with the mist.

I find a series of steps cut into the rock face beside the waterfall, and pick my way down slowly. They're wet and slippery from the spray. Scraps of vegetation offer the occasional handhold. I reach the bottom and cross to the edge of the gorge.

There seems to be movement down in the mist, but it's hard to tell. I don't see it where I look for it. It flickers in the corners of my eyes. An unwholesome smell hangs in the air, like anxious sweat, like old urine.

With a jolt in my gut I suddenly see myself pitching into the gorge, and I scrabble away backwards until my back hits the cliff behind me and I yelp, my eyes stretched wide.

It's not falling that I'm afraid of.

I sit there until my breathing slows, until my mind catches up enough to realize that I'm okay. I'm not afraid of falling. I get to my feet and try to brush the mist-damp dust from my pants. I remember a bridge.

I head to my right, keeping my distance from the gorge.

A plain stone bridge comes into view, maybe two metres wide, with low stone railings. I ease toward its centre, one step, another step. The smell is here, too, clinging with the mist to the lip of the pit. Again, a flicker of movement, and I twitch back from the edge.

I'm going the wrong way. I should go back. No, not back, some other way. But which other way? No, I'm right, aren't I? I should take the bridge.

I move farther away and sit on the ground. Maybe someone will come. Someone I can ask. Where the hell is Silvio Mondschein when you really need him?

And then someone actually does come, the same way I did. He has black hair and a thick black beard, more Semitic than Asian. Tools or implements of some kind clack together in the rough-woven bag over his shoulder.

"Are you all right?" the man asks. I can't tell what language he's speaking, but I understand him.

"Yeah, sure," I say. "Fine. Bit disoriented for a minute, that's all."

I'm lying. I'm afraid to walk across a *bridge*, for Christ's sake.

"Are you going this way?" he asks, gesturing toward the bridge.

And as he does the mist swirls and lifts. For the first time since I reached the cliff the way ahead is sharp and clean. Not a gorge after all. Barely more than a ditch. A thin stream bed, a minor tributary on its way to join the flow from the waterfall. And no gorges beyond either—just low green mounds, and a clear track between them into the distance. Even the bridge looks safer, its railings higher, its foundations solid as mountains.

"Um, yeah. Yeah, I think so."

He smiles. "Lovely day for it," he says, and continues past me. Along the ditch rather than across it.

"Yeah." And he's right. The day has grown quite lovely. "Thanks," I say as I start over the bridge.

Twelve

A CURL OF WIND THROUGH A HONG KONG HOSPITAL WINDOW.
Cool against my cheek.

I have an idea.

The land beyond the bridge seems gentler, no barrens or chasms.
Sweet green woodlands with easy slopes and clear passage.

I can't tell if the river I'm following is the same one as before.
All I know is that I'm heading upstream. It can't be the waterfall
river, then, because I was following that the other way. Downstream. Unless I got turned around somehow.

But I haven't come back to the waterfall, so that seems unlikely.

Unless I missed it.

I could ask someone, I suppose.

If there were anyone to ask.

If I knew what to ask them.

One evening I told Silvio Mondschein about Some Call Me Tim and
his panicked questions about eternity.

"What did you say to him?" Silvio Mondschein asked.

"I told him that it didn't matter, because I don't have a thousand years."

"How can you be sure of that?"
"Nobody gets a thousand years."
Silvio Mondschein sat back and smiled.
"You are so literal. It is quite charming, really."

Oscar Sliwka
York and Empire Bank (Canada)
Prairie Regional Office
York and Empire Bank Building
Calgary, Alberta
Canada

Mrs. Ying-min (Jasmine) Chen
[address]
Re: Jason Lavoie
Dear Mrs. Chen:
    This is to confirm the transfer, pursuant to your power of attorney, of sufficient funds from account number 6766-25850-994 (Jason Lavoie) to York and Empire Bank (Hong Kong) for the following purposes, to be administered by local bank officials until your arrival:

- local medical expenses previously incurred, ***** village, PRC;
- transportation ***** village to Shanghai PRC; Shanghai PRC to Hong Kong Special Administrative Region;
- hospitalization and medical care, Hong Kong Special Administrative Region.

    Your flight and hotel accommodation near the hospital have also been arranged, as set out in the enclosed itinerary.
    Please let us know how he's doing as soon as you can. Thanks.
Yours truly ...

I find a dirt road that seems to go west, and I take it. The sun gets higher, the trees thin out, the landscape gradually sheds it features. Soon the road is all there is.

After an hour or more I reach the top of a small rise and ahead on the right is a low stone shrine or hut, with a seated figure in front of it. Not a statue, exactly, but what looks like some sort of intricate mannequin, extremely well-crafted, with a withered nose and a ape-like muzzle. Some simian demigod. It looks like it could speak. And as I look for a place to plant a stick of incense—if I had some incense—it does speak.

One night at dinner Silvio Mondschein cuts off one of my fingertips. I lift my hand to emphasize something, and he slips his cigar-cutter across the table, smooth, swift, like an impatient bridegroom with a gold band. There's pressure, a splash of red on the tablecloth, then pain and the crunch of bone. The fingertip is in his breast pocket before I can speak. He carries on talking about the decay of tonality in Scriabin's piano sonatas as if nothing has happened, two fresh red dots on his linen suit.

The next morning it's back. The fingertip. I can't explain it.

Maybe he was trying to make some point.

I can't understand what the monkey-faced figure says at first. He seems to be trying different languages or dialects, looking for one that works. Some of it sounds like Sanskrit, or what I imagine Sanskrit would sound like if I had the slightest idea what Sanskrit sounded like. None of it is intelligible.

As the monkey figure works through his inner phrase book, a second figure ducks under the lintel and out of the hut. He has a bald head and a pig-like nose, round and flat, with forward-projecting nostrils.

"Form is emptiness," the pig man says. Him I can understand.

"Emptiness is form." Completing a thought to someone else, I suppose. Someone still in the hut. Someone with bunny ears and a puffy tail, probably. The pig man is carrying a rake.

"I," I say to the pig man—loudly, like a stereotype, like the Americans in the village, "would like to know"—I wave my hands vaguely around my head—"where this road"—pointing down —"goes" —pointing with both hands in the direction I've been following.

Why the pantomime I don't really know, since the pig man apparently speaks English. Or Mandarin. Whatever language I'm getting by on at this point. Like with the Semitic guy by the gorge, I don't seem to be able to tell any more.

"It goes the wrong way," the monkey-faced man says, picking up a stick and drawing absently in the dust. I guess now that I've spoken he knows which language to use. Whichever it is.

"Yeah, OK, but I'm talking to him now, actually," I say, pointing to the pig-nosed man. "Besides, how do you know which way is the wrong way? You don't even know where I'm going."

The pig man is stroking patchy chin-whiskers. "Form is not emptiness," he says.

"Thanks," I say. "That's very helpful."

"It goes the right way," the monkey man says. He has drawn a circle with his stick, in the dust.

"You can't know that either, can you. You don't know where I'm going."

He draws a line through the centre of the circle. "You didn't ask about you," he says, drawing another line through the first one, dividing the circle in four. He lifts his head and raises a pale eyebrow. "You asked about the road."

I shake my head and carry on the same way I was going.

After a few steps I stop and look back. "Let me guess," I say to the pig man. "Emptiness is *not* form?"

"No, of course not."

I turn away, then back again.

"No, of course it isn't, or no, of course I'm wrong?"

He smiles, lifts his rake to his shoulder, and ducks back in under the lintel.

"Gone beyond," the monkey man says. He snakes an 's' through the circle in the dirt, overlaying the cross with the conjoined teardrops of yin-yang. "Gone entirely beyond."

And the road snakes too, into a range of low hills.

That way.

From: miranda@telcom.net
To: osliwka@yorkandempirebank.ca
Subject: Jason—*URGENT*

Sleeve, your damn voice-mail is full again. There's a call on my machine from somewhere in China. They found someone there with my phone number. It sounds like it's Jason. He seems to be in some rural hospital, maybe unconscious. It's hard to understand the man's English. I've called Jason's aunt. Is there anyone over there who can help us sort this out? Call me asap.

I have to get out of the sun. My tongue is thick and sticky and my eyelids rasp. Everything around me is the same bone-bleached shade of beige.

Focus. Shade, water. Both. But eyeslits see only bone-shade. Wild monkey-thoughts jumping on the bed.

A mountain rises to heaven. Really just a big scabby hill, but I suppose if enough nature-poets call it a mountain ...

Maybe Silvio Mondschein was right. Maybe I should be careful what I read.

So I'm comin' 'round the mountain when I come, hoping for water, hoping to get out of the sun, but when I finish comin' 'round there's just more sun and no water and a sprawling concrete husk in a dead river valley.

A valley lost to dragons,
Forgotten by tigers.
Lost to dragons because the riverbed is empty and cracked.
Forgotten by tigers, who have passed on to green forests.

Monkey mind. Be careful what you read.

I shade my eyes and squint down at the structure. Linked concrete boxes open to the sky, roofs collapsed or carted away. An old warehouse or factory. It follows the curve of the dead river for more than a kilometre, jagged walls blazing white in the harsh sun and casting deep sharp-edged shadows inside.

Shade.

I start down.

Streaks of rust along the ground hint at an old rail-bed, at tracks and ties pried away for rice-paddy dikes and cooking fires and Mao's backyard smelters.

Or am I getting the chronology wrong? Were those before?

The path down to the valley floor is patchy with dead vegetation, and so uneven that again and again I almost lose my footing. A startled insect retreats into the shade of a half-buried animal skull. A small dog, maybe, or some sort of water-rodent.

I follow the rust-lines to a wide opening in a crumbling wall. Where doors once hung there are now brown, brittle weeds and a grit-edged wind, grasses decayed into fireflies.

I step inside, taking cautious shelter in the shadows of the broken walls. It is good to be out of the sun, but the dry air makes me cough, and the cough echoes into the next room and the next. Dust swirls through grey pockets of light, around empty corners and through frameless doors. I cover my mouth with my hand and filter my breath through my fingers.

Then I pause, still and wary. The echo.

Suppose the sound in the farther rooms isn't just an echo.

Suppose my cough has roused some parched local spirit? Some bony, desperate scavenger?

I have an idea.
    Here it is
    Emptiness.

There is little left here but concrete and half-light. In one room a three-metre expanse of wall has been hammered to pebbles, exposing iron rods that are bent outward but still there. In another room some of the roof's I-beams are gone, chipped loose from the tops of the walls. Such desperate, precarious effort—the climbing, the pounding, the risk of being crushed as the prize scrapes free and drops to the ground. The dragging home. The cutting up.

I walk softly on bare feet, on dusty, oil-stained floors. No more echoes. And yet still, in other rooms, around other corners, the suspicion of sound.

The babies keep staring at my eyes. Say something in French, Mister finky *French*-man. *Je ne sais pas*, I say.

In what was once probably a storage area, someone has piled rubble to reach an empty doorway up an empty wall. I pick my way up the slope—*réservé aux pèlerins* —and peer inside. Sunlight through empty window-holes, no floor. Gone entirely beyond. I pick my way back down. My feet hurt.

Concrete walls. How strange for a building to have concrete walls.

Emptiness at the centre.

Louisa leaning on her folded arms against a Montreal window ledge. Tiny, perfect moans in the growing dawn.

Funny the things you remember.

I walk, climb, squirm deeper into the wrecked building, down broken corridors, around rain-bleached drifts of debris. My movement raises swirls of dust as I pass, raises dust from the surfaces of my history's history. A car slams into an abutment as my eyes widen and narrow. A woman embraces a Chinese column, and dies. A man walks on into the wreckage of the past.

Did he work here? Is that why I'm here? Keeping accounts, turning machine parts on a metal lathe, loading boxes onto rail cars? Is there a room here where he hung his coat, where he ate cold noodles from a bowl with chopsticks brought from home? Are his traces still here—a flake of dandruff, an eyebrow hair, ash from a hand-rolled cigarette—in the dust that makes me cough?

But surely he came too late, the decades are wrong. Surely he was still skipping rocks on the Bow River when Mao leapt this particular leap.

The emptiness of a rock on pebbled ice, sailing straight through the house.
The emptiness of going entirely beyond.
The emptiness of a dead uncle.

Mama picks out simple tunes with one hand and holds a highball glass in the other. Melting ice cubes slowly cloud three inches of rye.

There is a rustling or scuttling two rooms over, in some windowless, airless interior. I've been careful to be quiet, to let dust and echoes lie, yet again I'm sure I hear something. Fireflies drift in the deepening shadows.
Which way makes you feel most apprehensive?
That way.

Report of Incident (translated and edited)

From: ******
To: ******

This morning a farm worker came upon a man unconscious under a tree near ***** River east of ***** Village. Denim trousers, cut off above the knee. No other clothing. No papers, but a yellow cloth-covered book: *Yijing* in English translation. Taken unconscious to the village doctor. Number on inside of his trousers, perhaps foreign telephone number. Still unconscious at time of report.

I'm sitting at the kitchen table eating jam from a jar with a spoon. It tastes like stale beer. It tastes like something French, something Chinese. Something Canadian.

Something.

I pass through an empty door-hole into a stairwell. To my right, concrete steps drop into the dark and disappear. A sawtoothed silhouette rises along the wall above, hinting at an option no longer there, torn away for fuel a generation ago. I trace the sawtooth with my fingers until I can no longer reach.

I turn my back and kneel on the top step. The rasp of my knees against grit echoes off of the scavenged walls.

"Perhaps it is naked women and ice cream," Silvio Mondschein says.

"Perhaps eat shit," I reply.

And I climb down backward, on my knees, one step at a time.

Acknowledgements

First and foremost, thanks to my wife and daughter for their love, support and inspiration, and, in my wife's case, for being the finest first reader an author could hope for. Without her clear-headed input throughout the writing process, this would have been a much clunkier book. Thanks also to those who provided feedback and encouragement along the way, including Grant Hurley, Graham Mariacci, Laura McRae, I.H. Smythe and Tracy Urquhart. Thanks to my parents for an education that fostered a love of the arts. Thanks to Michael Mirolla for his light but deft editorial hand. Thanks to the Guernica Prize judges—Cora Siré, Gabriella Goliger and E. Martin Nolan—for obvious reasons. And thanks to Guernica Editions for putting *Dead Uncle* out into the world.

Of the many sources I relied on for *An Idea About My Dead Uncle*, I would like to highlight the following: *The I Ching or Book of Changes* (Wilhelm/Baynes translation), published by Princeton University Press; *The New Emperors: China in the Era of Mao and Deng* by Harrison E. Salisbury, published by Avon Books; *China: A New History*, by John King Fairbank and Merle Goldman, published by Harvard University Press; *Streetlife China* by Michael Dutton, published by Cambridge University Press; and the factory floor sequence in Jennifer Baichwal's documentary film *Manufactured Landscapes*.

About the Author

K.R. WILSON was born in Calgary and lives in Toronto. *An Idea About My Dead Uncle* grew out of the journey he and his wife made to China to adopt their daughter, and the research into Chinese history and culture that it inspired.